Conquering
Starlight

Conquering Starlight

EMILY MAH

This one's for the girls: Tara, Makayla, Maycee, Breeah, Brynlee, and Averee!

And Kevin, a man with a big heart and truckloads of patience.

Part 1:

Liana

ONE

My hands clutched the edge of the desk in front of me as I watched an earthquake hit Mexico City. Aerial shots showed buildings collapsing into dust and incongruous lightning strikes flashing from the clear, blue sky. The picture shifted to a tsunami hitting the coast of India, an ancient seawall crumbling on impact as water shoved cars and buildings ahead of it like a great bulldozer. Next was a shot of London, where St. Paul's Cathedral was hit with a lightning strike that whited out the camera feed. When it cleared, there was only smoking ruin. Lima, Peru had huge waves pounding the cliffs of its coastline while lightning rained down like someone had parked a Tesla coil in the sky above it.

Siobhan O'Callan stood by the television, the remote clutched in her hands, eyes watching me intently. Her dark hair was still a little wild and her porcelain skin smudged with dirt. With a decisive squeeze of the remote, she switched off the feed.

"You get the idea, Liana," she said in her Irish brogue. "Earth is having a rough time right now. We've screwed it up royally." She cast her gaze down, offering no excuses.

"We" referred to her and the other angels in the room. Literal angels. Siobhan and the rest of the angelic order were tasked with protecting humanity from demons. They'd done their job well for thousands of years, but now all of those natural disasters were the work of fallen angels. Each of them a being who'd been benevolent for years, decades, centuries, or more, but had lost their grip, repudiated their covenants, and now wanted humanity to suffer.

I looked around the rest of the hospital conference room, at the tiny, motley crew of people who knew what was going on and had escaped alive. We were Earth's last hope. There were Siobhan and Mouse, representing the angelic order. Mouse was, as per her usual, skulking at the back, watching without being seen. There was Cecily, my college roommate at Princeton who had turned out to be a Sidhe. She was now much older than I—a side-effect of her being from a different realm, and thus a different timeline. I'd finished school a week ago. For her it had been twenty years.

My two best friends, Amy Blackhawk and Gina Rodriguez, from Taos, New Mexico, sat behind me. They'd been caught in the crossfire when everything went, literally, to hell. I was grateful they'd been with me and were now safe with the rest of us. For now, at least... With them sat my Aunt Cassie, who was wearing a babydoll dress and tie-dyed leggings. Her feet were stuffed into oversized fluffy slippers shaped like sharks, and her hair, which was still wet from the shower, was clipped up with a myriad of glittery pins. A sedate look for her, and a sign that despite her severe OCD and desire not to know about supernatural weirdness happening on Earth, she was holding up okay.

Beside me sat Corban. My... well, that was a long story. He was a hot guy who used to be an angel and was probably my boyfriend, but we hadn't had time to figure that out.

Finally, around the edges of the conference room were a handful of people with really weird coloring. Dark skin paired with light hair, hair that grew in tiger stripes of blond and brunette, deep purple hair. They had indigo eyes, yellow eyes, two-tone blue and brown eyes—the colors going in radial lines out from the pupil, which looks exactly as freaky as it sounds. All of them leaned against the walls, glaring at us, arms folded.

Before Siobhan could say anything more, the door opened and a coyote came trotting in with its ears and tail up. At the sight of the rest of us, it stopped, looked at me, and started to shift. Nobody flinched as it turned from a canine into a sixteen-year-old girl with dark olive skin, black hair, and tawny eyebrows and eyelashes. The black hair was a dye-job. As a coyote-shifter, she had the same odd coloring as the rest of her kind who were arrayed at the edges of the room.

A dark hand grasped the door before it shut and in stepped a black woman with neat dreadlocks tied back and an elegant, one-piece, ankle-length black dress that flared at the waist. She was new to me. We still knew so little about the coyote-shifters that I didn't know what to make of someone who wasn't their kind, but was in on their secret.

A middle-aged coyote-shifter with light purple hair and an annoyed frown, said, "Mother."

"Hello, Keira," the woman replied with a heavy French accent.

Aha, well that explained that. Though these two did not look related—Keira looked 100% white and this older woman had the kind of black skin so dark it was almost bluish—I'd known that the spell that created coyote-shifters struck at random, magicking unborn babies in families without any supernatural heritage, and I'd known that the spell altered their coloring, but I hadn't realized by how much.

The sixteen-year-old coyote-girl with tawny eyebrows came over and flopped down in the seat next to me. "Denise," she said to Keira's mother. "This is Liana. The half-turned vampire."

"Liana," said the woman, nodding towards me.

"You've got ten minutes," said Keira. "Say what you want to say."

"Then you go back to Earth, where mundanes belong," said the young guy with tiger striped hair. His tone was dismissive, disdainful.

That put me on edge. While I wasn't a mundane, most of the humans suffering on Earth were, and I'd assumed we were all on the same side here.

"Yes, of course," said Denise. She deferred to him, but there was nothing submissive in how she held herself. Her gaze showed that she considered herself on a level with everyone in the room.

I wondered if that was her being gutsy, or how people usually responded to that particular shifter. Right now the coyote-shifters had all the power. Their shape-shifting was just a curiosity. They had a power far more consequential: they were the only beings who could bring people from one realm to another. Hence they could work as "coyotes" in that sense of the word as well.

We and this room and this hospital the room was in, were in a nether-realm—a concept I didn't really understand. Aline, the teenage coyote who sat next to me, and was now doodling flowers on her forearm with ink, had tried to explain that it was a space between realms. It wasn't in any world and it consisted of an empty plain with one structure, this hospital. Only a coyote-shifter could get us out of here and back to Earth.

"Denise is my guardian, " said Aline, coloring in the petals of her flowers with black ink. "She's also an astrophysicist."

My heart lifted at that. Someone with a scientific explanation of what was going on was exactly what I needed.

Siobhan wheeled the television aside and Denise pulled out her cell phone, tapped the screen, and a projector came on in the ceiling. A hologram blinked into existence, a three dimensional diagram of what looked like a lumpy ball.

"I'll make this as simple as I can," she said. She spoke English with a French accent. "Humanity, as you all know, lives in a series of realms. The main one is Earth, but there are other realms... other worlds that some people can portal to with magic or supernatural ability or a phenomenon we, colloquially, call destiny. All these overlapping spheres—" she pointed to the diagram "—represent all these realms. They all connect to Earth and only Earth, not to each other, and are very similar to Earth. Some have magic, some have mythical flora and fauna, but the laws of physics more or less work the same in each of them and the people who dwell in them are all the same species. All Homo Sapiens. People who've crossed from one realm to another tend to have supernatural powers. The Sidhe—" She nodded to Cecily "—Fae, sirens, shifters—most of those individuals live in other realms and sometimes migrate to Earth, but are nevertheless humans, indistinguishable in a medical examination from someone like me."

One of the coyote-shifters—I didn't see which—gave a soft snort and Aline flicked her gaze to me in a subtle impression of an eye-roll.

"This applies to most supernaturals," Denise went on. "But then there are vampires and angels." She looked over at me.

"You are a bit different. You are humans possessed by disembodied spirits from the demon realm." She tapped her cellphone and another sphere appeared, colored red to contrast with the blue of the rest. It also stuck out from the lumpy ball, like it was trying to pull free.

"We don't know how these spirits are getting out of their realm with the portal sealed, and we don't know what these spirits even are. Human souls or... There's no science to explain it. Somehow beings with their own identity and motives are taking over human bodies." She looked at me. "People who can fight the demonic possession and retain their own sense of morality are powerful allies."

Well, I wasn't powerful. By not letting myself turn all the way vampire, I ended up with pretty much no supernatural abilities. I looked down at my hands, still grimy from the fight before I'd escaped Earth.

"Do we have any of the other kind of possession here?" Denise asked. "Any angels?"

Siobhan coughed softly and the woman's gaze swung to her, taking her in. Then she looked at me. "But you can always see them?"

I nodded. It was a rare trait for a non-angel, to be able to see angels even when they didn't want to be seen, but I had it.

"Fascinating. I also have no science that explains why people possessed by other-realm entities can be invisible, or not have reflections or any of that." She gestured apologetically at her diagram. "This is all I can tell you."

"That," I said, "is incredibly helpful."

Around us, the coyote-shifters grew restless. None of them liked me complimenting this woman. She gave them all an uneasy look, then said, "Well, the other thing I can tell you is that the demon realm does not appear to belong with these other realms. It's tethered to Earth, but it doesn't appear to have grown out of it, and it's trying to pull away. Right now the effects are disturbances in the barriers between realms, the creation of nether-realms, and increased cross-realm traffic, but over time it will destroy all the realms, Earth included."

"Doesn't belong?" Amy, my fellow-nerd friend, asked. I could hear her weight shift as she leaned forward.

Denise turned towards her. "All of the other realms are very similar to Earth. Same atmosphere and elements. But you take iron from the demon realm..."

I looked down at the three ferrum rings I wore on my fingers. "Ferrum" was what we called iron from the demon realm.

"It is identical to our iron according to every test we can perform," said Denise. "But different. Poisonous to anyone possessed by a demon, unworkable by a metalworker unless they have an ancestor who has been to the demon realm and back."

At that, my friend Gina shifted in her seat. She was a ferrum-worker.

"I mean," said Denise, "the differences, they go deeper but I'm trying to spare you the math."

"Thank you," said Corban.

"It's just not..." She frowned, searching for the words. "Not part of the same universe perhaps? I don't know exactly."

Several coyote-shifters rolled their eyes.

"I don't pretend to understand the prophecy that the tamer of demons—" she looked at me "—is going to be able to stop this demonic war with angels falling everywhere. The science says you need to somehow sever the demon realm from Earth and let the two go their separate ways. I wish I could tell you how to do that." She shrugged. "I can't. It seems something that a magic user would better understand. I know the war between vampires and angels has destroyed a lot of records, which means you don't have much to go on. But if I can help at all, please let me know."

"Thanks," I said. "Seriously."

"My brain needs a break," said Corban.

TWO

veryone else in the room seemed to agree. The coyote-shifters all started for the door, like schoolkids who'd heard the bell ring.

"Thanks Corban," said Gina, behind us. "My head was gonna explode, there."

Corban pivoted to me, his smile wry. "I am too confused to know if my head will explode or implode or what."

"Can Denise stay for a little while?" I asked the departing shifters.

Aline held up a hand. "Just, like, don't say anything. They probably won't throw her out right away."

Denise gravitated over to us, looking first to Aline who stopped doodling on herself and sat up.

"You all right?" Denise asked her.

"No... not really. We can't come up with any excuse to bring him here?"

I had no idea who "him" referred to, but I noticed that Aline cast a furtive glance at the door, as if to assure herself that all of her kind had left. She was talking about something in front of me that she didn't want them to know.

Her guardian shook her head. "If we sever the demon realm, the nether-realm will collapse. I'm not sure this place is any safer than Earth. We'll do our best to look out for him." Denise turned to me. "It's good to meet you."

Her expression was unreadable. I didn't see suspicion or warning, but I also didn't see warmth or acceptance. I wasn't sure whether to promise that their secret was safe with me or not, even though it was. Aline had saved my life numerous times and was the reason we were all safe.

"And it's good to meet you," I replied, getting to my feet, my muscles stiff. "You wouldn't happen to know anything about the last expedition into the demon realm? The one about three thousand years ago?"

"Somehow, it created vampires," she said. "It was only angels and fallen angels before that."

"Right," I said.

"But you want to know the science." She rubbed the corners her eyes with her fingertips. "Around that time, the ties between the demon realm and Earth got stronger. It ended up doing more harm than good, speeding up the time when the demon realm destroys all the other realms."

"Can we not do that this time?" asked Corban.

"Were you part of that expedition?" Aline looked at him.

Denise blinked in surprise. "You're immortal?"

"Kind of?" he said. "But not that old. That was a thousand years before my time."

"But he knew the guy who led that expedition," Aline explained. "Otuo... the angel I made fall who kind of started all this..." She shrank into herself.

"You," Corban reiterated, "did not make him fall. His weakness did."

"You know him?" Denise brightened.

Corban extended his hands, rubbing at the dirt in his fingernails. "This is all that's left of him... I, uh... I had to kill him."

"We didn't know his full story," I said. "We were hunting the vampire, Melanie, and he tried to team up with her. We had to kill them both."

Aline was focused on Corban. "You had to kill him? I'm sorry..."

"You killed both Otuo and Melanie?" asked Denise, eyes widening.

"They totally did, by themselves," said Aline. "Before we got there."

"But, you had powers then, right?" Denise was sizing us up again. "I'm sorry, but what are you? An angel?"

"Yes," said Corban. "But I overextended myself and I've lost my powers for now. I did have them during most of the fight, yes."

"Well, still..." Denise flashed us a smile. "You have my respect. And I have a request. If I could talk to a magic user, perhaps I can match up what they do with my science a bit?" Her voice went tentative.

"My roommate," I said, "Cecily... where did she go?" I cast my gaze around until I saw her standing at the back of the room, talking to Siobhan. "She's a magic user." I pointed.

"Ah right. I'll go speak with her, then." Denise nodded a goodbye.

Corban put a hand on my arm. With a jerk of his head he indicated the hallway outside and I nodded. Aline walked out of the room with us, but kept on walking when we stopped. There wasn't anyone milling around in the hallway. They'd all scampered off.

"Not sure how long this break is gonna be," Corban said, "but you wanna go back to our rooms?"

"Yeah, okay."

THE HOSPITAL HAD a wing of studio apartments, presumably to house the doctors and other medical staff that worked here—though there was no sign of those. They were comfy rooms, but odd as well. While they had things like regular beds and little kitchenettes in the corner of each, the carpets were avocado green, the appliances a violent turquoise blue, and the sheets were made out of a very soft fabric I could not identify. The logos on everything were written in a strange, swirly script that Corban told me wasn't Arabic, but that was what it looked like, and whatever cleaning products were used smelled like a cross between floral perfume and citrus. It wasn't an unpleasant scent, just a strange one.

We ducked into my room, alone for the first time in over a day, and I turned to face the guy I'd had a crush on for four years. The guy I might or might not be in a relationship with. Angels didn't do relationships, and vampires were their nemeses, but when I'd turned fully vampire four years ago, he'd kissed me to bring my soul back. It was a crazy move and should have killed us both.

But we'd survived, and we'd burned the demonic possession out of each other almost completely. I'd gone back to being a half-turned vampire. Corban had lost all of his angelic powers for a year. He ate and breathed and slept and aged like a human for that time, while I could walk in the sunlight without even the slightest sting.

The angelic order had separated us for that. Aside from our mutual attraction not really fitting into the moral rules of the universe, there was also the two thousand year age gap to consider. Corban had been born during the Roman Empire.

But last week, we'd reunited to fight the vampire, Melanie, and had kissed again. That happened in the middle of our last fight with her, and had given us an advantage. She'd swung at Corban, thinking he was still an angel, only to find out too late that he was a human. Corban and I hadn't had a chance to talk about it since.

Now we stood in my room, him with his hands in his pockets and his lower lip between his teeth. He looked like he was my age, or maybe a year or two younger and had blond hair, blue eyes, and very buff physique.

"Um... okay," he said, "you want me to start?"

"Sure..." I wasn't too afraid that he'd break my heart on purpose. He'd made it clear that he liked me. I was more afraid that he'd say or do something weird that I couldn't relate to. There was a whole lotta anthropological history and arcane philosophy crammed into this guy. He wasn't just some cute jock who'd smiled at me across the cafeteria.

He raked his fingers through his hair. "You kissed me to save our lives, or because you wanted to?" he asked.

"Both," I said. "If your life hadn't depended on it, I would have waited until after."

"Okay, cool..." He nodded. "So... you wanna go out sometime?"

"I've gotta go to the demon realm and save civilization," I said. "But if you wanna come..."

He chuckled, then stepped forward and pulled me into his arms, his body warm for a change. With his angelic powers, he'd been room temperature, which had been like hugging a mobile mannequin. A very strange feeling, and I strongly preferred him this way.

"There is no way," he whispered in my ear, "you're doing that alone."

Then he pressed his lips to mine.

For a guy who'd only ever been kissed twice in his life, he learned fast. The world blurred out and my knees went weak.

I put my arms around his neck and hung on for dear life as he trailed his fingers down my back.

I was the one to break it off. There was a lot about the morality of us being together that I was hazy on, but I was sure that anything beyond kissing was off limits. Corban still took his angelic covenants seriously, even if he didn't have the supernatural powers to go with them.

He looked into my eyes, his narrowing slightly as he opened his mouth to say something.

Someone pounded on the door and he let go of me, turning to see who it was.

"Hey," shouted Aline, "so, like, there's a problem."

"Worse than Earth being destroyed?" Corban asked as he opened the door.

Aline was leaning against the frame, her lips bent down at the corners. "So, you know how the people who went to the demon realm in the last expedition were, like, my kind, some angels, humans from the Nabatean civilization, and probably some magic users and stuff?"

"Yeah?" said Corban.

"We checked with all those groups. Nobody remembers or has any records of who sealed the portal. So we don't, like, have the spell to unseal it."

"How many portal sealing spells are there?" Corban asked.

She shrugged. "Nobody knows. Depends on the magical system used and the Oath syntax and whether the spell is tied to some kinda event. You know."

"No," I said, for what felt like the millionth time with Aline. "We really don't know this stuff. But if I understand you right, we're locked out of the place we need to go to save Earth, and we don't know who has the keys?"

"Right."

THREE

Aline looked ashamed, like we were her parents and had caught her sneaking out her window in the middle of the night. I didn't understand that at all. This wasn't her fault.

"I'm pretty sure Melanie would have recorded the spell," said Corban. "And we have her notes."

"If not," I said, "wouldn't the Citadel have a copy?" The Citadel was where the angelic order kept their archives on Earth.

"Um, so Amy's going through Melanie's notes," said Aline.

My poor friend Amy had a bachelors in anthropology but was, through circumstance, now the chief historian/linguist/ etc. for our demon realm expedition. She was the most qualified person in the group.

"I'll help her," said Corban. He kissed me on the temple and moved past Aline, into the hallway, and off towards Amy's room.

Aline watched after him a moment, then turned to me.

"Does Denise have any other specific insights into how to sever the demon realm?" I asked.

She shrugged. "No. There's not, like, a ton of data. There've only ever been three tamers of demons. One died, another one fell, and then there's you."

"Wait, three?" I said. "I thought there were two."

"The person who built the portal to the demon realm and Otuo, the founder of the angelic order are the other two," said Aline. "This looks like Judeo-Christian lore, so you'd, like, expect things to work in threes."

To her credit, she didn't add, "obviously" to the end of that.

"How is the person who built the portal to the demon realm a tamer of demons?" I asked. "That was pre-demonic invasion. What did he tame?"

"Coulda been a she. Um, so like, something evil got them to open the portal." She shrugged. "The original tamer... tamer's not a perfect translation. The original word is... like... the host of a symbiont, where it's real symbiosis. Not parasitism, which is what vampirism really is if you ask me."

For a kid who said "like" every other word, she had her basic biological concepts down.

"Anyway, they communed with something that was evil that got them to open the portal. And then demons came and made the evil worse. It's another form of the Garden of Eden story. Being tempted by something supernatural to bring evil into the world. It was a long time ago. Like... a hundred and fifty thousand years ago, maybe?"

"Anything else your kind knows about the history of the demon realm that pertains, here?" I tried to keep the irritation out of my voice.

"Other than you being the last ever tamer of demons? No. The stories of the first one were all passed down orally until someone wrote it down and so the details are, like, really vague. Just means you're our last chance, is all."

It was hard not to pound my fists against the wall. This whole endeavor to save Earth was like trying to do a mission to the moon with the high school science club. The absurdity was stifling.

Aline, true to form, seemed unruffled. "Like, so Denise is having some scientists and people brought in."

"She is?" I looked up.

"Yeah." Aline bit her lip again and nodded toward the far wall of my apartment.

That was where the window was; I'd kept the curtains drawn. The view made me uneasy, but at Aline's gesture I went over to have a look, pulling aside the heavy drapes. I froze with shock at what I saw outside.

The nether-realm was a broad, flat plain that extended in every direction with no discernible vegetation or animal life. There was no sun here, just a bright splotch in the cloudy sky that suggested a sun, but it didn't rise and set. Instead it wandered a random path. I did miss the sun. It had kept my vampirism at bay for years, though this soon after an angel's kiss, I didn't have to worry.

Now, the plain outside was swarming with people. They were setting up tents in neat rows with avenues between them, and lining up military machinery: tanks, it looked like, though they appeared to walk on mechanical legs rather than treads. Huge troop transport vehicles. Heavy artillery that looked like it was straight out of Star Wars.

"What in the..." I said. "Did you do this?"

"Keira portalled them in," said Aline. "I mean... we made it look like it was some magic users. Denise has been planning how to go into the demon realm for a while. She didn't expect a wave of fallen angels, but she knew the realm dragging on ours would be a problem. So... like, in all the human realms, there are a couple of peoples who know about and study the demon realm and are, like, technologically advanced. Denise had me and Keira ask them to loan us forces."

"This is amazing. Can I just ask why the rest of your kind is not all the way on board with this? Or am I misreading?"

Aline fidgeted with something under her shirt and looked away. "The others don't think the collapse of human civilization is their problem."

"Yeah, they're fun."

"Because they can go into any world they want, they just don't feel that this could hurt them."

"Sure, they're like vampires " I knew this attitude well. "They think because they have powers, they are above mere mortals."

More military hardware wheeled into view and parked in neat rows, and Keira, easily identified by her purple hair, directed them where to go.

"Vampires are awful," Aline agreed.

"It's not just vampires," I admitted. "It was a problem at the prep school I went to, too. Rich people thinking that the fate of regular people doesn't really affect them."

"So how come you're not like that? You're rich and a vampire."

This wasn't an easy topic for me. "My dad. He was always really firm about us not being better than anyone else. Kind of like Denise, I'm guessing?" It was notable that both Aline and Denise's daughter were the ones helping out.

Aline nodded. "If my kind knew half the stuff Denise says, she'd be dead. Well, maybe not dead. Like... exiled."

"Lovely."

"So, where's your dad?" Her eyes were wide with innocent curiosity. She didn't know.

"He got killed by vampires."

"I'm sorry."

I shrugged, having nothing else to say on the matter. Him being dead was one of those immutable truths. There was no new perspective or new idea about it that would change the simple fact that the world was still spinning, and he wasn't on it. I guess that's what making peace with loss is, giving up on the anger because it only hurt me and changed nothing.

Aline pulled something out of her shirt and looked at it, something shiny on a chain. I craned my neck and saw that it was a plain ring, like the ferrum rings I wore. "What's that?" I asked.

She fidgeted with it some more. "I married my boyfriend before I left LA."

"Oh." Now I knew the "him" she and Denise had been talking about.

"I mean... it gets him away from his abusive dad. Getting married is the fastest way to get emancipated."

"A legal marriage when you're under age emancipates you?" This was not the kind of thing I knew anything about. In my social circle, people usually didn't marry until their late twenties or early thirties, after the prenup was negotiated and signed.

"Yeah. Denise gave permission for me and his mother gave permission for him. There wasn't time for anything else with the end of the world coming and stuff."

I nodded. Boy did she look young. She really was just a kid with doodles on her arm and a lost look in her eyes. Her shoulders were tense and uneasy.

"Sounds like a clever fix," I said.

"My kind wouldn't let me, like, take him to safety."

"Sure." Though I wondered why that mattered. Aline portalled whoever she wanted whenever she wanted.

Her eyes glistened a little. "If they knew I was dating a mundane... it's not allowed, you know?"

Ah... "Sorry to be dense," I said, "but how does your kind punish one of your own? I mean... what can they do to you? It's not like a prison can hold you."

"They can hurt or kill Micah."

"Oh, right." That made a sickening amount of sense. "I take it he's the boyfriend... husband?"

She nodded, blinking back tears. "You probably think it's stupid of me, being married at sixteen."

"I think..." I chose my words carefully. "One of the guys I dated when I was your age turned out to be an evil vampire who ruined my life, and I probably wouldn't have made that mistake if I'd been older."

"Right."

"And the other guy I kissed as a teenager turned out to be an angel, which is complicated. I'm not sure I'm old enough to have any real advice for you, because I'm still working through all that. Just don't... don't worry if things don't work out with this guy. Unless we fail here, you two have your whole lives ahead of you."

She nodded, looked down, and dropped the ring back inside her shirt.

Despite the gesture, she was clearly all-in with this guy, which meant that it was a good thing that she was here, working on our expedition.

On impulse, I reached out and hugged her, finding she was a skinny, bony little thing who had a slight canine smell, like well groomed fur. She stiffened with surprise, but then hugged back.

"So we have military help," I said. "And they know their way around the demon realm?"

"As well as anyone does. You can't map it. It's, like, all black with just glowing huts."

"Okay..." I'd been drinking information out of a firehose for over a day, now, and it was all so weird.

"The dwellings," she went on, "like, float around on blackness. So they're moving in relation to each other all the time. Between that and the stars above... I mean, that's why they call it the Starlight Kingdom. Just looks like stars as far as the eye can see."

"Glowing huts?" I asked.

"Yeah, it's populated. Super populated. Millions of people at least."

"But you've got details about how it looks."

"That's, like, all I know. Oh, and the portal there is marked by a stone arch on their side, on top of a really steep stone pyramid."

"Okay."

"That glows."

"Right."

"I dunno, maybe all you need to do is knock down the pyramid." She shrugged.

"If I do that and it doesn't work, can I still reach the portal and get out?"

"I dunno. Maybe?"

I made myself look out the window again at the military amassing. Do not, I told myself, focus on how hopeless this is.

Someone knocked on the door and a moment later, Amy burst in. "Corban," she said, "just lied to me. You said angels don't do that."

FOUR

My friend Amy Blackhawk wasn't the dramatic type. That was Gina Rodriguez's thing. (Gina had come into the room right on Amy's heels and looked ready to strangle someone with her bare hands, but that didn't mean the situation was serious. Amy's scowl meant the situation was serious.)

I looked back and forth between them. They both had the dark skin and turquoise jewelry that marked them as Southwesterners. These two had been nice to me since my first traumatic day at Taos High. Me being a dork, a rich girl, and possessed by a demon didn't seem to affect our friendship, even when it meant they got dragged into a nether-world by werecoyotes. They were very, very tolerant people, so when they got upset, I paid attention.

"Corban is hiding something," said Amy.

"Hiding what?" I asked.

Aline looked back and forth between us, one eyebrow raised.

"About how much he knows." Amy shook her fist. "There's a passage in Melanie's notes he's not translating correctly, and he knows I know."

I'd never known Corban to be evasive when people's lives depended on him, and my first impulse was to defend him. Relentless practicality hit a split-second later, though. How well did I know Corban? Here I'd just condescended to Aline, telling her not to be too committed to the guy she'd fallen for as a teenager. Was I any better?

"I'll talk to him," I promised.

"What, you believe that an angel is lying?" asked Aline. "Your own boyfriend?"

"Maybe?" I headed for the door; Amy and Gina both stepped out into the hall ahead of me. Aline looked at us, then took a step and disappeared, portalling away.

"So you believe me?" asked Amy. She was about six inches shorter than I was and had to throw her head back to meet my gaze.

"Of course," I said. "Why would you lie about this?"

"You don't trust Corban? Seriously?" Gina's tone still had anger in it, but it was bleeding away.

"I want to trust him," I said, "but I don't always understand him. You guys, though? I trust you guys with my life. So tell me what exactly is up."

Gina gave Amy a triumphant look, as if to say, "See, I told you."

Amy's smile was rueful. "There's a passage in Melanie's notes that talks about the Nabatean expedition into the demon realm," she said. "Which is exactly what we need."

I nodded, relieved to hear she'd found it.

But Amy shook her head. "Corban's not translating it right. He's hiding something about it."

"Well, let me see if he'll hide it from me," I said. I gave my friends each a hug. It was our standard good-bye these days, when any conversation might be our last.

CORBAN WAS IN his room, the door open just a crack. The way he looked up when I pushed my way in told me he'd been expecting me.

Which meant what? I wondered. Were we about to have a fight?

From where he stood in the middle of the kitchenette area, I guessed he'd been pacing. And despite the gravity of the situation, I couldn't help but pause, take him in once more, and wonder for the millionth-plus time why a guy this gorgeous had given up his immortality for me.

I had to focus. "You made Amy mad," I said, trying to keep my tone light.

His expression didn't soften.

That wasn't good.

I slipped inside and shut the door behind me. "What?" I asked.

"She was asking about some stuff I needed to think about."

Okay, I thought.

When he looked back at me, I saw fear in his eyes. I'd seen him within seconds of certain death, so I knew he could be afraid, but I'd never seen fear quite like this. It normally didn't stay with him. It was a fleeting visitor, but this fear was eating him from the inside.

And that made me afraid. "What's wrong?"

"It's nothing."

"Corban—" I cut myself short and took a moment to choose my next words carefully. "Did you lie to Amy? Did you mistranslate something on purpose?"

"It's... not what it seems."

"That's a yes or no question," I said.

"Okay, hold off." He looked me in the eye. "Do you trust me or not?"

"I trust you until you give me reason not to. Did you lie to my best friend?"

He blinked a few times, then cast his gaze to the side. "Technically, yes."

"Well, don't do that. Tell her that you'll tell her what it means later. Or tell her... I don't know."

"I'm used to being able to disappear to get out of conversations," he said. "Just, 'Oh, this is awkward, I'll go poof now.'"

"Which isn't all that honest either."

"Now that you're making me think about it, sure. Fair point." He nodded. After a moment's pause, he went to sit down at the little table that served as a dining table/study desk.

There was another chair across from him, and I slipped into it with a slight creak of the metal joints, grateful that we weren't squaring off against each other anymore. "Will you tell me what's in Melanie's notes?"

He ran his fingers through his hair. "So... okay, we've got to handle this delicately."

"Handle what—"

"Hang on." He held up a hand and looked around his room, scanning the upper corners where the ceiling met the walls.

Surveillance. He was checking for surveillance. Another thing about him losing his angelic abilities meant that he still didn't know how to sneak around. Again, he was used to being invisible.

"Can we go for a walk?" I asked.

"Yeah..." He all but bolted out of his seat.

I let him precede me out the door and down the hall, then through a set of double doors that took us outside the hospital, into air so still that it felt like indoors. We were at the edge of one of the military encampments. Corban stopped dead in his tracks and stared.

"Denise got us some friends," I said.

"Denise did?" He looked back at me.

I nodded.

The soldiers were a racially diverse group pitching spacious-looking tents. Those out and about glanced up with friendly expressions. We nodded and smiled back. The language they were speaking wasn't familiar to me at all, but then again, I was no linguist. Nobody paid much attention to us as we started around the building and towards the edge of the their camp.

We rounded the corner to where there was just flat plain that stretched off every direction.

"Okay," I said, "so what did you find?"

Corban cast his gaze around once more for good measure, spending an extra moment to scan the walls and roofline of the hospital. "The Nabateans have an account of some visitors arriving before they began their expeditions into the demon realm."

"Visitors from where?"

"Just... another village to the south. Nothing strange about that. The thing is, those visitors figured out there was a portal to the demon realm in the Nabatean city of Petra based on some writing they found on the buildings—writing that it appears was removed."

"Uh-huh," I said.

He held up his tablet screen. On the display were the familiar curly-cues of the writing that was all over the hospital.

"So what are you thinking?" I asked. "That the race that built the hospital has access to the demon realm?"

"Coyote-shifters built the hospital."

"And we know they had access to the demon realm. They were there for the expedition. How is this a big deal?"

"This is evidence they'd been in contact with the demon realm before those expeditions. Think about it. We know nothing about the coyote-shifters. Nothing other than what they've told us. Who knows what they think or believe or what their agenda is?"

"They're helping us amass this huge army so we can go into the demon realm. Why would they withhold information if they had it?"

"They don't like us."

"They're arrogant supernaturals," I said. "It's nothing."

Corban gestured around at the unnatural flat plain. "That's not nothing when we're under their control. Look, we thought we knew what Otuo's deal was. He was the oldest guardian angel, but then he fell and decided to hate humanity. Then we find out that he was married to Gamlat." Gamlat was the original vampire, who we believed had fled back into the demon realm a few hundred years ago, destroying her notes and records beforehand.

"That changed everything," said Corban. "He wasn't just a loose cannon of hate anymore. He was willing to work with vampires to open up the demon realm again. We don't know whom the coyote-shifters are allied with and whether they've got some bigger agenda."

"Aline said—"

"Aline seems like a good kid, but she's also one of them. Young people like that? They act rebellious sometimes but deep in their bones, they're gonna do what they've been raised to believe is right. Think about it. If the coyote-shifters want the demon invasion, or angel war or whatever you want to call it, to wipe out human civilization, this is the best way to ensure nobody stops them. They've got everyone who's got a shot at it trapped here." He gestured around again.

Oh... I thought. Right.

FIVE

I'd been living on the edge ever since angels started falling back on Earth. I had been pushed beyond what I thought I could endure already, so the thought that all the risks I'd taken might have played right into the hands of an enemy? That was more than I could handle. I doubled over with my hands on my knees and gulped some deep breaths.

"Why would anyone want to bring on the apocalypse?" I asked. "Do we think they work for Satan or..." There weren't concrete records of a fallen angel named Satan, but a lot of members of the order and Christians like me believed in him, some as a concept and some as an actual guy.

"We need to know more about the coyote-shifters and what they want," said Corban. "Kind of hard to do that if they might be plotting against us and nobody else in all of human existence has any records about them."

"The Citadel would."

"But they'll be written in this language." He pointed to the curly-cues. "I know a ton of languages, Liana. This one isn't related to any of them."

"But if the coyote-shifters really are on our side, we have to at least act like we trust them," I said. "Without showing trust we could get into a misunderstanding that makes all of this pointless."

"Yeah but—"

"Aline," I said. "We talk to Aline."

"I'm not sure we can trust Aline."

I held up a hand. "Maybe her upbringing influences her a lot, but think about it. Think about who she's already proven herself to be."

She'd been the one to find us when Melanie made a move against me. She'd supplied us with ferrum weapons and told the group of us (back when Otuo was still one of us) all about who the coyote-shifters were. That meant divulging ancient, tightly-guarded secrets. Even if she wasn't loyal to us and our cause, she hadn't been terribly loyal to her kind either.

"She'll help us," I said. "I believe that."

"I'm just worried that the shifters may already be onto us," said Corban. "You getting told by Amy that something's up and coming to me. You and I sneaking out of the hospital. If they have surveillance..."

"What do you want to do?"

He clasped his tablet in front of him and cocked his head at me, contemplating something.

"What?" I pressed.

"You talk to her? Alone? I'm no good at sneaking around."

"I'm no spy," I said. "I don't do sensitive negotiations. I have exactly twenty-two years of life experience, and I don't think the two years I spent learning to walk and talk are all that relevant here. You're the ancient being. You've got the wisdom."

"But none of the basic skills," he said. "I don't know how to not act suspicious when I walk up to someone."

"I don't either."

"You get the concept," he said. "Whether or not you can execute it, you've at least had to think about it. I haven't for thousands of years."

"You used to read minds," I said. "Or-or sense emotions at least. You know how people think."

"Uh, no," he said. "Reading minds doesn't help you understand how people think. Quite the opposite."

I took another deep breath of oddly still air. Don't psych yourself out, I told myself. Pretend it's just a delicate conversation with a professor about how they graded your paper. Aline wasn't that scary, after all. Not in human form, at least. "Okay," I said. "Fine in theory, but she portalled somewhere and do we trust being able to text her? Or do we worry about her kind tapping our phones?"

This had been a major issue back on Earth. Cell phones were convenient, but they were not secure and our enemies had tapped ours.

"Get someone else to text her?" Corban suggested. "For an innocuous reason?"

"Sure..." But who?

Why couldn't life just be simple again? I was tired of living in a paranoid schizophrenic's worst nightmare.

And then it hit me. I could enlist the help of, not a paranoid schizophrenic, but a person living her own worst nightmare. My Aunt Cassie. I looked up at the hospital and got an idea.

In Taos, Cassie had lived in an Earthship—a type of sustainable house that wasn't connected to the grid. Could that be of use to the coyotes with their hospital that was not just off grid, but slightly off-reality? "Maybe Cassie can say that she sees something wrong with... their water cisterns or... whatever they have here."

Corban nodded. "Yeah, that works. You go find her. I'm gonna... I'm gonna go back to researching." He kissed my forehead before heading off.

I started the other way around the hospital, and luck was with me. Cassie was over by the far entrance and seemed to be wandering by herself, which she did sometimes, "to hang onto what shreds of sanity I have left," she joked. I started towards her, hoping I didn't represent a looming sanity-shredder bearing down.

"Cassie?" I called out.

"Mmm?" She stopped meandering and turned to look at me.

"I need to talk to Aline alone, and I need your help." It was hard not to giggle at the sound of "Aline alone." Either I wasn't too traumatized to have a sense of humor, or I was losing my mind completely. Under the circumstances, what did it really matter?

"Aline?" Cassie chewed her lip. "Is there any reason you can't just text her?"

"Yes, but you probably don't want to know what it is."

"Say no more." She shook her head and got out her phone.

"Look," I said. "I'm sorry about all this weirdness."

"The way I see it," she said, "is that I'm alive and a lot of people on Earth aren't. I have you to thank for that."

"That is kind of you. Okay, so here's the deal." I explained my idea of coming up with an off-grid technology excuse to text Aline.

"And you want me to act like a batty lady obsessed with stuff like water filters because Aline won't question it?" Cassie tapped away on her cellphone.

"Well..."

"I am fine with that. I really am. The water filters are on that side of the hospital." She pointed a boney finger. "I'll ask her to meet there. And then I'm going to go hide so I don't hear whatever it is you guys discuss. Good?"

"All good," I agreed.

THE WATER FILTERS were by what looked like a pair of blast doors, on a side of the hospital that did not have a major military encampment. Probably because it also had no entrances or exits and the soldiers would be using things like the hospital cafeteria, labs, bathrooms, and conference rooms.

Aline showed up by herself, looking pretty much the same as she had half an hour earlier.

At the sight of me, her steps slowed a little and she raised her eyebrows.

I was probably looking nervous, because I was nervous. The more minutes ticked by, the more the feeling that this whole realm was a prison I'd never escape closed in.

She walked up to within about ten paces of me and stopped. "Is Cassie here?"

"No," I said. "I have a question."

"Yeah?" She drew the word out long, no doubt wondering why I was acting cagey. Especially after our heart-to-heart within the last hour.

I took a deep breath and dove in. "There's evidence that people were in contact with the demon realm before the last expedition, and that evidence is written in the language that's also all over your hospital. You guys aren't hiding any records written in that language from us, are you?"

"Huh?"

"Whose language is that? The curly-cues?"

"Um... we don't... like... talk about it."

"I'm sorry if this is paranoid of me, but you guys do want to stop these angel wars, right? You guys wouldn't hide the spell that seals the portal to the demon realm from us, would you? You're sure it's not in any records you have dating back to that time?"

"I... don't know. I want to stop the angel wars, yeah."

"And the rest of your kind may not care, but they wouldn't block us, would they?"

She rubbed her eyes, a gesture that spoke of exhaustion, confusion, and stalling for time as she considered my question. Finally she said, "I'm not, like, all in the know with them. I'm not old enough."

"Who were the people who originally spoke that language? The first coyote-shifters?"

"No..." Aline shifted her weight, clearly stuck between a rock and a hard place.

"I really don't want to dig around in your kind's secrets," I said. "You've gone above and beyond for us. It's just that if your kind wanted to imprison us here, they've got it all set up to do that."

She blinked, then her eyes widened.

"But we assume for now that they don't," I said.

"I... I don't think..." With a burst of nervous energy she shifted into coyote form and ran a rambling path around me, ears back, tail down. After a moment, she shifted back. It was strange how she could do that with her clothes on. "If they do want to trap you here..." She was fighting back tears.

"People deserve the benefit of the doubt," I insisted. "If they're doing the wrong thing, that'll become obvious eventually, but if we accuse them of doing the wrong thing unfairly, or even just assume, we risk making this situation worse..."

"Sure," the girl agreed.

"So." I took a deep breath. "Is there anything you can tell me that you feel comfortable sharing?" I wished there was a place to sit down, but the ground underfoot wasn't just flat, it was hard as a stone floor. "I understand if there isn't," I said, spreading my hands in a way I hoped was calming.

She heaved a sigh. "That swirly language belongs to the people who didn't just create us, they enslaved us," said Aline.

"I do not mean to trivialize that at all," I said, "but does that mean you can read the writing? And would you help us check to see if there's a portal-unsealing spell written in that language?"

SIX

"Yeah, I can read it," said Aline. She wrapped her arms around herself, clearly scared.

"Can you think of a reason why your kind would want human civilization destroyed? Not just be indifferent to it, but want it to happen?" I asked.

She shook her head.

"Is there anything in the history of the people who enslaved you—"

"No, that was, like, thousands of years ago. Nobody cares about them anymore. They died out... like... right after that demon realm expedition. Not that that, like, killed them. They'd been dying out for a while at that point. Coyote-shifters were the last major thing they made."

"So you're worried about going against your own kind," I said, "because they could have leverage over you, I get that."

Aline bobbed her head from side-to-side in a noncommittal nod. "I mean... Saving the world is the right thing to do. I just... I hate how it always hurts me to do it. I had to leave Micah alone. He just sent me a bunch of texts saying he hates me and wishes he never met me and I can't tell him the truth about where I am and why I disappeared. He doesn't even know what I am." Tears were pooling in her eyes again.

"I'm sorry," I said. "Secrets are hard."

"You got to tell your two best friends yours."

"Yes," I said. "And my aunt. I've been very lucky."

"And I don't know if my kind will, like, care if I go help you find the spell. I just don't know what their deal is, or if they even have a deal. It's not like we usually work together and coordinate stuff. I gotta be really careful."

"I understand."

"But I need them not to look at me too closely. If they find out I'm in love with a mundane... Tobias thinks I belong with him."

"Who's Tobias?" I asked.

"The guy with the tiger-stripy hair."

"Who's, what? Ten years older than you at least?"

"We're not supposed to date outside our kind. He's the closest to me in age, and if he finds out about Micah, he will definitely kill him. Tobias is... he's like that."

"I am really sorry to hear that your kind does the megalomaniac abusive thing too. I'd hoped that was confined to vampires. I know you've already taken huge risks for us. If you can't help me here, I will understand. I was thinking we search the Citadel for records in this language. If your kind were made by a major civilization, then they've gotta have some records of it. Maybe we find the answer without having to ask your kind."

She swiped at her eyes with the back of her hand. "Okay. Sounds good. Let's go do that. Let's save the world." She squared her shoulders.

"Can I just say that you're amazing?" I reached out to give her another hug, surprised at how tightly she squeezed me back. "We would all be dead without you."

"Don't speak too soon," she muttered.

Fair point.

"THE CITADEL ISN'T controlled fully by the order anymore," Siobhan explained to us when we found her outside the conference room and hauled her outside to the water filters. "The order and the fallen are fighting over it. Breaking in is the only way. The problem is, if you're hiding from coyote-shifters while you do this, I can't go with you. They can track demon carriers."

"Not Liana and Corban," said Aline. "Ever since you two got together however you did, your demon connections are really faint. They get stronger over time, but right now they're weak."

I tried not to blush about that, especially not when Siobhan looked me over with slightly narrowed eyes.

"Let's get your friends," Siobhan said to me. "Let's do this fast while things are still chaotic and militaries are moving in and such. Those are good distractions."

FIFTEEN MINUTES LATER Amy, Corban, Gina, Aline, and I stood with Siobhan in the broom closet, and I tried not to be amazed at how universal brooms and cleaning supplies were to humanity. That was beside the point at the moment.

There was no reason for Gina to be there, except that she would not let herself be left out. The last thing I wanted was to put another friend in danger, but the thing about sneaking around was that she had a barrel handy to hold me over. All she had to do was announce our plan and that'd torpedo it. Not that I thought she'd actually do that, but the implicit threat signaled how badly she wanted not to be an outsider looking in on this heist.

Amy knew the layout of the Citadel archives—Siobhan, despite being an angel, was no scholar and had probably never set foot in ninety percent of the archive space, while Amy had studied the entire complex.

Corban was a seasoned fighter who, since he also couldn't be tracked by the other coyote-shifters, was the logical person to go in as our protector. And I was along because I was who Aline trusted. From the hundred dollars I'd given her when I thought she was just a starving girl in the Midwest to our heart-to-hearts and hugs, we had a bond now.

There were a million ways this could go wrong. The most obvious way was us being discovered and the coyote-shifters not being happy that we were sneaking around on them. I leaned on Corban here, with his long-life experience. "You do the best you can with the information you've got," he'd said. "And yeah, sometimes it goes wrong. There are no guarantees."

Since my friends were putting themselves at risk on my judgment call, I was going with them. An emotional decision, I knew; I was the tamer of demons. They would need me for the expedition. But I was able to tame my vampiric demon and keep my soul by keeping my moral code, and that meant not standing aside when my loved ones went into danger.

Amy was showing Aline a map of the archives, which extended for miles under the city of Istanbul. Parts of them had been flooded with gas and blown up, but apparently the miscellaneous section, where the records of languages lost in antiquity were kept, was still intact.

"To be safe," Siobhan was saying, "you should wear fireman's gear. Oxygen tanks and masks and such so that if it's flooded with gas, you can still breathe."

"But that won't make you completely fireproof," said Aline. "Fire resistant is all. But yeah, like, that would be good."

"The archives are organized by language family, where known," said Amy.

"Well, this language would probably be assumed to be Levantine," said Corban. "A lot of Earth's writing systems got their start in that region, so that's where you see the most diversity, and it has a calligraphic structure that's reminiscent of Arabic."

"And none of the angelic order knows the language?" asked Gina. "Isn't that suspicious?"

"It's old," Aline reiterated. "Like, really old."

"Three thousand years?" I asked.

"More like fifty thousand."

"That is way old for a written language," agreed Amy. "That's, like, ten times older than all the other written languages." She peered at Aline.

Who only shrugged. She clearly didn't want to talk about it.

"Wouldn't Otuo have known it?" asked Gina. "Why would he not catalog it with the other known languages?"

"He definitely didn't do that," said Amy. "There's nothing like this in the known languages list."

Corban held up a hand. "Otuo or someone may have cut a deal with the coyote-shifters to let them have the language to themselves."

Aline nodded. "Yeah, that could totally be possible."

I examined that and decided it made sense. When there was a powerful organization, like the coyote-shifters, that wanted something, it was sensible to believe they'd gotten that something at some point. And given they were former slaves, there were all kinds of non-nefarious reasons for them to want things, and for someone to want to help them.

"Why didn't Otuo preserve the portal sealing spell, is what I want to know?" Gina demanded.

"For all we know, he did," I said. "And then he fell and we killed him and if he has a secret stash of information somewhere, we have no idea how to find it."

Everyone looked to Gina to make sure she didn't have any more questions or accusations to lob. She held up a hand to let us know she didn't.

"So," said Siobhan, "the main thing to watch out for in the archives are fallen angels. The ones you see tearing things up on Earth, those are the flashy ones, but there are ones that choose to be more subtle. Those are who you'll find in the library."

"Subtle how?" I asked.

"They like to mess with you on a personal level," said Corban. "Like, when a building's collapsing, some fallen angels feed on the mass pain that causes, and some will go into the wreckage and find the little kids crying for their parents and make them more scared and confused and traumatized. Makes for a better-tasting kind of pain."

"Because it's sick?" asked Gina.

"Yeah." He nodded. "There aren't enough of us in this group to create great, mass pain, so we'll probably get someone who wants to torture each of us to maximize individual pain."

"But they will still collapse the library as a finishing move," said Siobhan.

"Noted," said Amy. "So what do we do if we find one of these angels who wants to torture us?"

Corban and Siohan exchanged a shrug.

"Oh, there's no defense, really," said Siobhan. "I guess what I meant to say was that just because a fallen isn't pulling the roof down on you right away, they're still dangerous and can still hurt you."

"Okay then." Amy rubbed her eyes. "Well... cool. You guys ready to go?"

SEVEN

An hour later we were fully dressed in firefighter gear that seemed just a little off to me. I suspected non-Earth origin, but it fit well and was even comfortable. I wore everything but the face mask (no need to deplete the oxygen tank unless it was necessary), hood, and gloves. I didn't bother with the gloves because I was holding hands with Corban.

Amy and Gina had first aid kits slung over their shoulders.

If there'd been time, I'm sure Corban and I would have joked about having one last makeout session before we portalled so that we'd stay hard to track, but we didn't get even a second alone. Also, I wasn't sure if Corban would find the joke funny, or if he'd think I was being too forward. I strove to be a good Christian girl, but what kind of standards did my angel boyfriend even have? I prayed that we'd get a chance to talk to each other about these things.

Still, his hand felt good in mine as we watched Aline, the last person to rejoin us, slip inside the closet. She looked at its dimensions with a frown.

"So how is it you're able to see where you'll emerge from a portal?" I asked her. "And how is it there are portals everywhere?"

"The nether-realm, like, basically wraps Earth," she said, "so there are portals to Earth everywhere here, and vice-versa."

She paused and looked at me. "I can tell where I'll emerge because I can, like, see through the portal. To me it kinda looks like a gateway. It's a really faint view, but enough to get my bearings. So we're gonna need to portal in and out of the nether-realm a few times before we get there. Just stay with me, okay?"

I had an image of myself in fireman gear just popping into existence in the downtown of some random city, but decided to believe Aline was savvier than that. She motioned for all of us to walk towards the back wall, and we did.

Only to have the wall disappear and a tropical beach take its place. A strong breeze whooshed past us, echoing loud in my right ear and pushing the wisps of hair I hadn't managed to get up into my ponytail off my neck. The familiar smell of saltwater and and the crash of surf was a surprise. This was an uninhabited beach, as near as I could tell. There were no footprints or anything to indicate other humans had ever been here. The sun felt amazing.

Aline trudged across the beach like she was crossing the street, and we all kept pace so we didn't fall behind.

The beach faded and was replaced with the familiar, flat plain of the nether-realm. The hospital was off on the horizon, with its military encampments looking like little swarms of bugs from this distance.

That faded and we were in the baking heat of a desert, the Sahara, perhaps? It looked like the film representations of it, at least. I'd never seen much of it in real life, aside from a holiday weekend in Morocco with my dad.

We trudged through the sinking sand, my quad muscles starting to burn from the exertion and my fireproof clothing blessedly well suited to shedding heat. The sun beat down like we walked under a great oven element, and then it was back to the nether-realm.

This time I had to look around for the hospital, and saw it in the distance behind us. It was strange how we'd walked a straight line, by our reckoning, but it was a crooked line across the nether-world.

"'Kay," said Aline. "Here we go."

The bleak plain gave way to pitch darkness and oppressive, moisture laden air. At least it was cool moisture.

A light winked on and Aline held her flashlight aloft, illuminating the walls of a tunnel encasing us. We all stopped walking. She reached into her pocket for a device that looked like a geiger meter and scrutinized its screen. "The air here is breathable, obviously," she said, "but there's, like, no ventilation. It's not moving at all." She held up her device and turned to Amy. "Which way?"

I hoped this didn't mean we could have walked into non-breathable air. If I'd suffocated with an oxygen tank and mask strapped to my body, I would have felt like a complete idiot.

Amy had already switched on her own flashlight and was scrutinizing the walls, which were stone and rather slimy, like those of a natural cave. I was guessing that wasn't a good thing. Archives were supposed to be dry and preserve the contents from things like mold. This place seemed more suited to being a mushroom farm.

"Um... kay," said Amy, turning her flashlight down a corridor that seemed unnecessarily long and narrow. "If we assume pre-Levantine, we go that way. There should be a door on the left before too long."

We all rearranged ourselves as best we could in the strait confines—there were several "I'm sorry"s and "excuse me"s, but eventually Amy was in the lead and the rest of us trailed behind, our footsteps sounding loud as they echoed off the walls.

In the distance came a rumble and a slight shudder through the floor.

"That doesn't sound good," said Gina.

Aline lifted her sensor device. "So far, not a problem. I'm seeing the natural gas levels rising, like, a little bit... pretty negligible, though. This place is big enough it'd take a while to flood it."

Amy had reached the doorway and knocked on it. "Um... there's no door handle on this thing."

Next to me, Corban muttered a mild curse word. He didn't properly swear—and neither did I. One thing about being ridden by demons, we had to be more straight-laced than the average person. "It'll be locked from the inside which isn't an issue for angels because locks don't work on us. I didn't even think about it, and neither did Siobhan."

Aline looked back and forth between us, then dug something else out of her pocket. "Lemme through."

"There's no lock to pick on this side," said Amy.

"It's a magnetic lock," said Corban. "You need a specific kind of magnet to open it."

"Mmm... okay." She chuckled as she knelt down and pressed her tool to the gap under the door. There came the sound of scrabbling on the other side. "So, like, these little automatons throw the tumblers or move the latch or, like, whatever."

"You just keep tech like that in your pocket?" I asked.

"Maybe. Hey, I'm reforming. I try to be a good person."

I wasn't aware she'd ever been a bad one.

The door swung open, and tiny, spidery figures that moved too fast for me to see properly went skittering back into Aline's tool.

Aline reared back. "There's a lot more gas in here than there is in the hallway. Get your masks on."

We all obeyed and pulled our hoods and gloves on as well. Now our suits were sealed off, which meant we could survive a natural gas blast long enough to portal out. I took a deep breath of the cool, astringent-smelling oxygen from my tank. It was a little like the air of the nether-world.

"And, like, be careful with sparks," Aline went on, her voice a little muffled by her mask. We had radio links, but fallen angels might be on the same frequency, so we kept those off and shouted instead.

Amy shouldered her way into the room, followed by Corban. Once it was my turn to get inside, I noted with a sinking feeling that the place was big enough to house several olympic sized swimming pools. Stacks upon stacks of shelves, all walled off with protective glass, ran the length of the place.

"Um, my lock picker-thingy won't work on those," said Aline, pointing to how each glassed off area had a pin pad to open the lock.

"So we break the glass," said Gina, holding up what looked like a small blacksmith hammer and a railroad spike.

"No," said Amy. "I told you not to bring that stuff. We break the glass and expose the artifacts to the outside air, and they're lost."

"We don't break the glass," said Gina, "and we never figure out how to open the portal or learn what the hell Liana's supposed to do and the world ends. Priorities?"

"No, just this civilization ends," said Amy.

"Gotta side with Gina," I said.

Amy pulled out a little, cell-phone looking device. "We can use this with the keypads, barbarians." With a jerk of her head, likely meant to flip her ponytail, she began stalking down the aisle, her gaze passing over each set of stacks as if she knew what she was looking at.

We all shuffled after her as Aline kept watching the meter. "There's a gas leak somewhere in this room," she said.

"But we opened the door," I said. "That should diffuse it a little, right?"

"Doesn't seem to be doing that."

"Here," said Amy. She pressed her cell phone to the keypad, and nothing happened. No lights, no beeps, nothing. She tried again.

"I told you the system would be down," said Gina.

"We can't break the glass."

"Sometimes you gotta care about tomorrow more than the past," Gina replied. "'Cuz the future's where we're going to spend the rest of our lives."

"Did you seriously just quote Plan 9 From Outer Space?" Aline asked.

"Hey, you know it?" Gina grinned.

I did not know it.

I could see Amy wrestling with the reality of the situation, analyzing it from all angles. Finally her shoulders slumped. "Go ahead."

"Try not to create sparks," Aline reminded her.

"Cool fact, ferrum doesn't spark."

"Those are ferrum?" I asked. That metal was beyond rare.

"Ferrum plated." Gina positioned the spike against the glass and struck it hard with the hammer. Spiderweb cracks shot out in all directions. She struck it again and they grew more dense; turning the entire pane white. Then she lowered the spike and smacked the pane itself with the hammer and the entire thing shattered, shards flying inwards. Apparently they kept the artifacts at negative pressure. Or maybe they kept the air supply low for fire suppression?

Aline darted forward and grabbed a clay tablet off the shelf, despite a squeak of protest from Amy. "This, I can read this. It's worded a little weirdly, but it's definitely the same language."

"Well," said Amy. "Get reading then. We've gotta find the right records, and then we'd better get out of here before this place blows up."

Another bang sounded, not as far away as the last one, and it wasn't an explosion. It was someone dropping a heavy object. With icy fingers clawing at my heart, I turned to see who had found us.

EIGHT

I reached for Corban's hand to warn him, but he'd already spotted the danger. Gina had spun the other direction to check for threats from that direction, which was smart. I wished I had instincts like that.

Aline ducked down and hid. I noticed she grabbed several clay tablets and was reading them, setting them aside, and grabbing more. It was destructive, but it was the right call in the moment. I was surrounded by people who knew how to handle a crisis.

I did not lead the curve on this. For one thing, I'd looked straight at Aline, the person who we most needed to hide. I hoped that my mask and hood obscured my head enough so that it wasn't obvious I'd done anything but look at the stacks.

The better thing to do was look at what loomed near us, a man with long, white hair and ebony dark eyes.

Angels ascended from all age groups; this one had been an elderly man when he'd answered the call to serve humanity as a guide and protector. Now he'd given up that call and given in to something much worse. The black eyes were the mark of being fallen.

He wasn't throwing lightning bolts or making the floor shake right now, though. He was just standing there, staring at us. A manipulator, then.

"Where did you come from?" he demanded.

"None of your business," Corban replied, his voice muffled but still audible. "I serve God and I am on His errand."

Those, I suspected, were angelic fighting words.

The man laughed. "God sent you to the obscure languages section of the archives?"

It took a major force of will not to look at Aline again. She was our exit. We were safe as long as she was here with us.

Even if this fallen knew that Aline was with us and was a coyote-shifter, he probably wouldn't know that her real superpower was the ability to portal between worlds. Nobody else from the order had known that until Aline had chosen to disclose it to a small group of us a week ago.

I stepped back so that Aline could see my profile more clearly, and adjusted my hood. Out of the corner of my eye, I saw her check to make sure her hood was sealed to her mask. The fallen angel needed to not see her face.

Corban adopted a casual stance that managed to show his bulging biceps. In other circumstances, it'd be hot. Now I worried that he was poking the bear.

The fallen angel smiled a smile that looked like the rictus of death. "You're looking at ancient pre-Levantine languages. Whyever might you be doing that?"

"Order request. It really doesn't concern you. Some of us are trying not to destroy everything from the past."

"Such as pre-Levantine languages?" The fallen pushed some strands of his long white hair back over his shoulders. "You've killed all the Nabatean vampires, so why are you still interested in that region?" He lifted a snow-white eyebrow. "Or do you think Gamlat's still alive?"

I was morally certain she was still alive, but to the rest of the world, she was missing and presumed dead.

There was a different problem brewing here, though. He might not know why we were interested in the Middle East and Nabatea, but if he could confirm that we were interested in the region, the fallen might turn their gaze in that direction. Our expedition did not need armies of fallen angels marching on us when we tried to reach the demon realm portal.

Corban was silent. He'd said he wasn't comfortable with negotiation, but did that hold true even with his own kind? He'd never been invisible to them.

Then again, he'd been one of the oldest and most senior members of the order. Angels had shut up when he narrowed his eyes at them.

The fallen angel took a step forward. "So who do we have, here?" he asked.

I held my hands up to ward him off. "Gamlat wasn't Nabatean," I blurted out. "She was... something else."

The fallen gave me an amused grin. "I see."

I should have left this up to Corban.

I was young and clueless and overmatched and... the fallen had stopped walking forward. I'd stalled him. If I had a measure of control over this situation, I needed to use it.

"She wasn't Nabatean," I repeated. "She didn't even look Nabatean, think about it. She was from a much older race."

Now, this stuff was true, and there was a good chance I'd regret divulging it, but I couldn't think of any such reason right now. Corban wasn't stopping me either, so I kept talking. It was best to mix it up a little, though. "She pretended to be Nabatean." Belatedly, I remembered to let my walls down and allow my emotions to spill out. All of us knew how to wall our minds against being fed on by angels, but that gave away the control that we had.

Corban's attention had snapped to me. I hoped and prayed I hadn't screwed this up.

"Calm down," he ordered. His tone was a little off. It sounded concerned, but not the way he sounded when concerned.

I hope that meant he was playing along.

"They probably already know this!" I shrieked, my mind shifting into overdrive. "The signs were all there. Gamlat pretended to be from Nabatea because that's where the earliest vampire demon myths originate, but anyone who thinks about it will know she was from—"

"Don't," Corban argued, cuffing me with a cupped hand that made a sound far louder than the resulting sting. "What's the matter with you?"

Okay, now he was definitely playing along. No matter how desperate I made him feel, Corban did not hit people, and he would never, ever hit me.

I let myself sound hysterical. "He's going to kill us anyway—"

"Keep your head on straight. Pull yourself together."

A set of hands clamped down on my arms. "Yeah," said Gina, "pull it together Maria."

Amy, I now saw, had stolen over to where Aline sat and was pulling tablets down off the shelf and handing them to Aline, then taking cell phone pictures of the ones Aline hadn't gotten to yet.

"We're all dead anyway!" It was easy to get into this role. I completely believed what I was saying. "And then they're going to find the secret compound in North Africa and—"

"Are you trying to get us killed?" Corban demanded.

"Just... let him get it over with. Let him kill us." I was spewing pure terror now.

The fallen angel began to chuckle. "Oh, I'm sorry, is my delay in killing you making you nervous? Terribly sorry." My fear began to drain away as he fed on it.

I felt calmer, and more confident. I also knew what he was doing and what the stakes were. I let him have my fear, knowing I could generate more in a heartbeat, and as long as I could keep him feeding... "Oh... I feel better now," I said.

Corban didn't have his emotion-sensing, fear-feeding abilities anymore, so I had to tell him what was happening.

"Sorry..." I said. "What was I saying? I didn't give away..." I clapped a gloved hand over my mask.

"Maria, you really aren't winning any Academy Awards here, are you?" Gina goaded me.

"A vampire compound in North Africa seems unlikely," said the fallen angel.

"It is!" I said, far too quickly. "It was a lie. Right! Totally a lie." I let more fear go coursing through me. "I mean... you know... The truth is, uh—"

The white haired angel stepped towards me.

Now I let the fear flow strong. "N-no... honestly—"

He took another step towards me and I squirmed out of Gina's grasp and fell to my knees on the floor, which was hard on the soft flesh under my kneecaps. It hurt something awful. I was going to have bruises if we survived this.

He took some more steps towards me as Corban nudged me discreetly forward.

Oh, right, the goal was to avoid him stepping close enough to see Amy and Aline at work. I crawled on my hands and knees towards him. "I wouldn't lie to someone such as you," I said. "I swear."

"You are a pathetic, lesser being."

Really? I thought. How generic was that? "I am," I said, groveling.

But his eyes grew darker and he drew himself up to his full height. He'd sensed the dip in my fear when I'd allowed myself to be amused. Why couldn't I be more petrified? Had my life gotten so messed up that I saw moments of humor in situations like this?

The angel's fingers sparked.

And that's when the air caught fire.

NINE

Someone, Corban I assume, grabbed me from behind as the whole world tilted and we fell into a void.

Then I was alone, falling endlessly. There was no sound of air whistling past my ears, no sense of there being a bottom I would hit. I was an astronaut in orbit around the planet, or so it felt. I'd be in a free fall until the end of time.

And then I hit the ground, hard enough that I almost screamed. I would have screamed if I hadn't hit so hard. As it was, I squeaked in a pathetic way. My leg was twisted under me and I found myself looking up at the hazy sky and dim suggestion of the sun that signaled the nether-realm.

Fire-masked faces poked into my field of vision as my friends looked down at me. I let out a deep breath.

"Did everyone make it?" My voice was still muffled by my mask.

Amy pulled her mask and hood off. "Are you insane?" She started cracking up.

If she was laughing, then everyone must've been all right. Nevertheless, I rolled onto my side to look for Aline.

She'd already thrown off her helmet and mask and was standing, still jittery, her eyes dilated with fear. I pulled off my mask and noted that the air smelled like char. "You okay?" I asked her. "That was amazing. How'd you get us out so fast?"

"Yeah," Corban agreed. He'd knelt down beside me and was helping me sit up, squeezing my leg to check for breaks.

I didn't think there were any, but there were bruises that made me wince.

"You okay?" I repeated to Aline.

Slowly she nodded. "You," she said, "were amazing."

I rolled my eyes.

But the others piled on, pulling away their masks and hoods so they could speak more clearly.

"You so were," said Amy. "You stalled and we got a bunch of stuff recorded."

"And it was hilarious," Gina added.

"I was almost convinced you were losing it," said Corban.

"Did you get what we were looking for?" I asked.

Amy hoisted one of the portable first-aid kits. Its soft sides were bulging. "I stuffed what I could in here. I took pictures of what I could. Aline read what I could. The section wasn't that big; maybe we got what we needed."

"We did," said Aline. She pulled a tablet out from inside her suit and held it up. "The spell to unseal the portal."

Motion in my peripheral vision made me turn my head. Tobias-with-the-tiger-stripe-hair, appeared, his arms folded across his chest, his gaze stormy with anger.

WE WERE MARCHED overground to the hospital, rather than portalled. I didn't have a problem with that, per se, other than that it was a mark of how deeply in trouble we were and my leg hurt. Aline, however, refused to look cowed. Actually, she looked furious. Normally she had a shy demeanor, but she walked with her head high and her eyes flashing.

There were going to be fireworks, that was certain, and there was nothing I could do. This was coyote-shifter business.

Corban gripped my hand tight in his. We'd removed our gloves, hoods, and masks and shut off our oxygen tanks. Gina and Amy looked slightly more bewildered as we hiked along.

I tried not to chuckle at how Tobias was the one out of breath. Everyone else was used to long hikes, and while the air in the nether-realm was still and tepid, it wasn't particularly thin. Gina, Amy, and I had spent enough time living in the high altitudes of Taos to keep fatigue at bay.

As we approached the hospital, the first thing I noticed was that the armies were on the move, packing up their tents, calling out instructions to one another.

"What?" said Aline, noting this the same time I did. She took off at a run, transitioning into coyote form as she did so that she could speed along faster. As a tinier figure in the distance, she went human again and began talking to the soldiers.

I couldn't hear her, but I could see that she was calm. She wasn't shaking her fist or yelling. Her head bobbed this way and that as she spoke to them.

Apparently she knew their language.

Tobias ground his teeth, a sound that always made me cringe, as three more coyote-shifters materialized around us. One of them was Keira. The other two were ones whose names I didn't know; one was a woman with black skin and blue hair. The other was a heavyset man who looked like an albino East-Asian, except his eyes had brown and blue radial lines.

With an exchange of glances, they began to portal us; the world shifted to freezing cold tundra, but before I could get too uncomfortable, we were in the lecture hall where Siobhan waited, her head bowed and her expression defeated.

Corban, Amy, Gina, and I all exchanged glances.

With a gust of cool air, Aline appeared as well.

"Before you get all lecture-y," she snapped, "I'm gonna tell you what we found."

"Aline—" Keira began.

"We found the spell to unseal the demon realm. We got it out of the Citadel. That's all we were doing, okay?"

Tobias whipped around and slapped her across the face, hard enough that it sounded like a thundercrack.

Aline staggered back, clutching her nose, blood dripping down her chin. Then she went for him.

Siobhan intercepted Aline, bringing them both crashing to the floor hard enough that I winced, but she pressed a hand to Aline's cheek, healing away the injury while the other coyote-shifters all recoiled in shock.

"Okay..." I said. "Everyone calm down. We figured out how to unseal the portal. We weren't trying to pull anything. We just figured—"

"Quiet," Keira told me in a harsh whisper.

But my temper wouldn't let me do that. I turned to Tobias, who stood smirking after hitting Aline."Why are you angry with us?" I demanded.

"Like you don't know," he replied.

Aline was back on her feet, and she was still furious, but also in control. "We didn't go to Q'tal, okay? Let me present what we found, Tobias." Her tone was even. There were no stammers, no insertions of "like" anywhere. It was telling that Siobhan slipped behind her, as if expecting protection from her.

A six hundred year old warrior and field commander hiding behind a sixteen-year-old girl.

"Aline, we do not discuss these matters in front of them," said Keira, gesturing at us.

"Them?" Aline shot back. "Mere mundanes? The ones who might save the world? There's a time to hide and a time to trust. The fate of all the realms is at stake."

"Their world." Tobias shook his head.

There it was, the assertion that our problems were not theirs.

"Listen," I said, "we have no interest in prying into your secrets or the history of this civilization that made you. Anything you have from them that you want to keep from us, that's fine. We're just trying to stop the demon invasion. We appreciate your help; we're all humans here, right?"

Tobias laughed.

"Oh," said Aline, "so we don't remember any of the the lessons of the Q'tallans, do we? Seriously? You're not going to care about the rest of humanity?"

"We all know why you feel an affinity for humans," said Tobias in a tone that was meant to be scathing.

No, I thought. No, no, no. Aline had done one thing to save one human she cared about. They couldn't throw it in her face now.

But Aline bristled in a way that made me fear she was about to shape-shift again. "I am human."

"Okay, wait, stop," said Keira. "Let's focus here. Aline, please tell me you didn't go to the Citadel and tell the fallen where to look for the spell to unseal the portal?"

"They didn't know that's what we were after," I said. "And they destroyed that part of the archives, so they'll never know."

"But we can go to Petra now," said Corban. "Get the portal open and get through and then that's all the help we need." Clearly he didn't feel confident enough to broach the topic of getting us out again.

Tobias's smirk had gotten more pronounced, though, and he grabbed Keira by the hair. "Or maybe we just leave everyone here and get on with our lives."

Keira blinked in shock at his assault.

Too fast for me to fully grasp what was happening, Aline went into coyote form and leapt at the two of them. They all disappeared.

All of them. There were no coyote-shifters in the room with us now.

"Where's Denise?" I asked.

"Banished," said Siobhan. "I hope just banished. Honestly, I think she may be dead. Once you guys left, the other coyote-shifters got uptight about the military pouring in and feared they'd figure out who had the power to portal them. Keira tried to hold them off, but Tobias took Denise to have leverage over Keira and... it's been ugly."

"Uh..." said Amy. "Aline will be back right? Someone will, right? We're not trapped here, are we?"

This was a fair question.

TEN

"Well..." said Siobhan into the silence. "They'll have to come back eventually. They won't want to leave us in control of this hospital..."

Corban, however, leaned back against the desks and slumped his shoulders forward. It was terrifying to see him look vulnerable.

I wrapped my arms around myself. Everything we'd sought to avoid had happened, and worst of all, it was my fault. I was the one who'd gone to Aline; I hadn't meant to isolate her and put her at odds with her own people. She'd given us so much.

There were also hundreds of soldiers outside whom I'd just trapped here, away from whatever governments or peoples who might rely on them.

"Hey," said Gina, putting a hand on my arm. "We'll be okay. Aline will be back. Or Keira. Or another one of them. They can't all be that bad, right?"

"Think about it," said Amy. "There was a specific secret they were hiding and they're all going to be mad at us for poking around."

"Right," said Corban. "They're hiding whatever technology their enslavers used to enslave them." He rubbed his eyes. "Which I can see why they'd be skittish about. They don't know us, so they were worried we were going to do to them what that society, the one that spoke that language, did. Aline can insist that we didn't go to... wherever their main archives are, but they probably don't believe her."

Well, when he put it that way, it was an obvious thing for them to fear. We'd been having to make so many plans so fast that I hadn't figured out that wrinkle.

"They're going to want to kill us," said Siobhan. "Wipe us out and forget we existed."

"No," I said. "It's a waste of time and energy to worry about them doing that right now. We should get prepped to go to Petra, so that if Aline gets back, we're ready to roll on out."

"But—" Siobhan began.

I held up a hand. "If she shows up five minutes or five days from now, we need to be ready to move."

"Yep," agreed Gina. "That's what we need to do."

"Agreed," said Amy. "There isn't much we can control, so we do the best with what we've got. We use our time to pack and prepare."

Corban rubbed his arms. "Valid point. Okay, let's do this."

Everyone turned and headed out the door.

SIOBHAN WENT OUT to talk to the militaries, revealing that she knew one of them spoke an offshoot of French and another spoke an offshoot of Uzbek. They were no doubt descended from small populations from these countries that had portalled at some point in history.

Gina got to work ensuring that every scrap of ferrum in the hospital was handed over to the militaries and loaded up on vehicles. If we were leaving, then we were taking it all with us.

Aunt Cassie was the least affected by it all. I don't think it was because she didn't care, but because she chose not to care. "We have food, I have stuff to do. You get on with your stuff," she said. In other words, me asking her to do anything more would only stress her out.

So I charged my borrowed phone, packed up my duffel bag, loaded said duffel bag into one of the SUVs, and then set about helping the military clear out all the food in the kitchen. They, it turned out, had little freezer units in their supply transports, so we packed those full of frozen goods and stashed all the cans of food in bins that would ensure they didn't roll around.

Once the kitchen was emptied, we joined those cleaning out the pharmacy, piling all the medicines and medical supplies into the supply transports as well.

I went around to all of the vehicles to make sure they had fully stocked first aid kits.

Then I went to the lab, but found that the scientists Denise had brought in had already packed up their research. With such a huge group sharing the work, the hospital was already stripped of supplies and feeling as hollow as it had when I'd first arrived. It was like the end of every year of school when I moved out of my dorm—I even had a pang in my chest.

And yet, I'd only been here for a little over a day and we might never, ever leave this place.

Outside, the splotch of light that stood in for the sun had moved across the sky and dipped towards the horizon, which meant nothing but made me feel like the day was over. When I rejoined the military encampment, everyone was sitting around on their bags of gear and such, eating a meal of beans and rice that made the air smell like saltwater and protein.

I accepted a bowl from a soldier and took an eager bite, unaware until right now of how hungry I'd been. The food went down so fast that I barely tasted it and my stomach growled and tore away at it like a ravenous animal.

The great crowd had gone quiet. There was only the sound of footfalls and the scrape of metal utensils against metal bowls. A steady stream of people who'd finished eating filed into the hospital and I followed along, washing my bowl in the kitchen, drying it, and then stacking it in a rack that would be taken back to one of the transports.

And then I was at loose ends, which I could not handle. This was prison to the nth degree.

There was no sign of Corban or Siobhan or my friends, so I wandered back to our studio apartments, where I found a door opened a crack that shone a line of light into the darkened hall. Voices emanated from inside.

"—can't handle this," Amy was saying.

"Well, don't lose your mind. It's not fair if you get to and I don't," was Gina's rejoinder.

"Nobody is losing their minds." That was Siobhan. "I will imbibe the crazy from your minds."

"You can do that?" asked Amy.

"No lying," Gina reminded her.

"Just, be calm. It'll be all right."

"Can we do crazy things?" Gina asked. "People are allowed to do crazy things in dire situations."

"Like what?" Corban asked. "Go lose your virginity?"

That question shocked me, because it seemed like such an un-angelic thing to say.

Siobhan was laughing. "I think you're the only virgin in this room, Corban."

"Uh, don't make Liana turn fully vamp," said Gina. "Please. That would be inconvenient."

"He would fall too," said Siobhan.

I'm not sure what I did that alerted them to my presence, but between Siobhan and Corban, the group had hundreds of years of experience being aware of eavesdroppers. The door jerked open and Siobhan blinked out at me. "Oh, hi, Liana," she said with an awkward strain in her voice that might have been acting, or might have not.

Amy and Gina both cracked up anyway.

"Right, we'll leave you alone, then." She pushed past me into the hall with my friends trailing behind her.

They gave me amused smiles, and my face grew so hot that I wondered that my head didn't explode from all the blood rushing to my cheeks.

Corban, at least, did not look mortified. He stood in the middle of the room, brows slightly together, as if trying to discern what I was thinking.

I tried not to fixate on how his muscles shifted under his loose-fitting shirt, or the way the light from the window gave his skin a slight glow.

As much as I didn't want to stand in the hallway being a dork, I didn't want to go into his room and shut the door either. Odds were, my friends were watching me, forming opinions. Running away would be rude. I had no idea what to do.

He came to the door and beckoned me in.

My cheeks were still burning as I ducked under his arm and he shut the door behind me. "Sorry about that," he said. "Siobhan's an ancient Celt. Bawdy doesn't even begin to describe it."

"That wasn't bawdy," I said, as I turned to face him.

He stepped away from the door, towards me. "Right. Look... I've lived long enough that I'm not going to try to guess at what you're thinking. I'll just ask. Why did that embarrass you?"

"I assume she was making fun of me for not having enough control not to..." I couldn't finish the sentence, and the way Corban cocked his head made me think that he found that strange.

We were Christians, though. We didn't go around talking about this stuff in depth did we?

"Clearly you have control," he said.

"I got fed on by a vampire for weeks. I didn't have enough control to keep him off me."

He looked away. "Well... I'd like to think what you and I have is different from that. For me it is."

"Sure. I just... sometimes I miss being that close to someone and... I'm sorry to go there right now. I shouldn't have even brought that up." I averted my eyes from him.

"Liana, listen." He stepped up to me and put his arms around my waist, drawing me in close and pressing his lips to my forehead. "I want—"

Something flew through the air past us, close enough that I felt the whoosh of its passing. By the time I'd turned far enough to focus on what it was, Aline had shifted into human form, and she did not look good. Blood dripped from a gash behind her ear and there were claw marks on her hands and arms.

She got stiffly to her feet. "Um, hey," she said. "Let's move."

ELEVEN

"You're alive," I said.

"Yeah, but we gotta move now. The others are gonna be here any sec." Aline pivoted on her heel and limped out the door.

I moved to follow her, but not before Corban could duck in front of me and give me a long, lingering kiss, followed by a whispered, "I want what you want." Then he let me go.

I didn't fully understand what he meant, but this wasn't the time to stop and discuss the matter.

I dashed out the door and into the narrow hall with him on my heels. There was no sign of Aline, but the residential wing was near the main entrance, so it was a few strides and a turn before my hands smacked into the cool glass, shoving the door aside so that I could exit.

The militaries were all formed up in ranks, vehicles at the ready. Aline was limping far ahead, shouting something I couldn't quite hear. She came limping back and repeated it in English.

"Follow me out on to the plain, and then be ready to get dropped straight into Jordan. We leave, now!" And then she was in coyote form once more, running out onto the plain.

WELL DAD, I thought as Corban helped me into one of the SUVs we'd liberated from Melanie. Hope this isn't the end of us. The other vehicles were starting their engines and Siobhan clambered into the driver's seat, with Mouse taking shotgun. She'd kept such a low profile, I'd almost forgotten she was here with us. No doubt, that was the idea.

Gina and Amy came running from the hospital to join us. Aunt Cassie waved at me before climbing into one of the military transports. Apparently the militia was fine with that. Nobody stopped her, at least.

My friends piled into the bench seat behind mine and clicked their belts on with shaking hands. I turned to make eye contact with each of them, the awkwardness of ten minutes ago now ancient history.

They both smiled as best they could, and I smiled back as best I could.

Then I turned back around, buckled my seatbelt, and shut my eyes. We were behind a pair of tanks, but otherwise at the front of the caravan. No matter what happened, everyone wanted me to get through the portal Aline opened. Hope you'd be proud of me, Dad, I thought.

I'd never offered a thought in Dad's direction before. For years it had been too painful to think about him, a reminder of my own foolishness and the dire consequences that had resulted.

It was still just as painful. That hadn't changed and it had been long enough that I knew it never would. I also knew now that I could look into that empty space without being destroyed. Not completely, at least.

Corban reached over, took my hand, and rubbed his thumb along the length of mine, causing small jolts of sensation. I gave his hand a squeeze, unsure whether I was returning the affection or asking him to ease off a little.

"Ready?" asked Siobhan from the front seat. The alligator-like tanks in front of us had begun to move and she put her foot on the gas.

We started at a crawl, but the tanks kept on speeding up and so did Siobhan. Soon we were flying across the empty plain of the nether-world, vehicles stretching out behind us. The tanks ahead of us winked out of existence.

"Oh... wow," said Corban. "I didn't think about coyote-shifters being able to do it that way."

"Go Aline!" said Gina. "You rock, girl!"

Up ahead, Aline stood with her hands up, eyes shut, and body translucent. She was out of phase, I guess you could say, supernaturally holding the door open for us from this world into the next. Gone was all pretense of magic users opening a portal.

She was showing her powers to the entire militia. I watched her until the world went black.

The SUV burst out of the nether-realm and its tires hit paved road. Stars winked to life overhead and desert stretched in every direction. Rock formations and cliffs rose around us, and scrub brush dotted the landscape. The moon was a great white disk overhead, casting its silvery light over everything.

I looked back at my friends who both craned their necks to look out their windows, taking in the dark desert all around.

The climate control came on with a whoosh, though from where I sat, I couldn't tell at first whether it was air conditioning or heat. Only when I smelled the warm air did I know. Deserts did get cold at night. New Mexico had taught me that.

Siobhan let the SUV drift to the shoulder of the road. "I need to see if the others showed up."

"What others?" I asked.

But Siobhan only stared intently out the back window and said, "We can't risk radioing. We have to assume the fallen may be tapping the transmissions."

The rest of the motorcade rushed on past and I twisted around in my seat to look at the vast army of ground forces that had just materialized on the unsuspecting world.

Corban had his phone out. "Still no major disruptions in Jordan," he said. "No lightning storms or earthquakes or anything like that. Closest disaster sites are in Israel."

So I wouldn't see the catastrophes that came with the end of the world first-hand? The coward in me was grateful for that. The video feeds had been enough. Seeing that damage in granular detail? The people displaced, the children orphaned and crying, the young people maimed and broken... that was more than I could handle right now.

I'd been to Jordan before—and even Petra. My dad had worked long hours, but like typical rich people, we'd had some fabulous vacations. Needless to say, my prior visit had been during the day and we hadn't brought an army.

I looked in the rearview mirror and saw headlights coming at us from the distance, past where our vehicles were materializing out of the portal. I twisted around in my seat again and stared at another fleet of cars coming down the road. "Who are they?" I asked.

"Who are who?" asked Amy.

That was my first clue.

"Angels," said Siobhan. "A legion of them. I told them to assemble near here before I went to the nether-world with you lot and told them to be on the lookout for anyone materializing out of thin air. Helps that there are rather a lot of us. Everyone else up ahead knows what to do. I briefed them." She was grinning with relief though, and I couldn't help but do the same.

This was a major boon for us, having angels to guard our approach, and it was a neat trick of pre-planning that Siobhan had pulled off.

Sure enough, as I watched, the fleet of cars overtook us, swerving onto the shoulders to form two columns, one on each side of the army—about half of which was through the portal by now.

The knot in my chest unravelled itself. This was perfect. Angels had the power to share their invisibility if there were enough of them. Now the human world wouldn't see this crazy military group materializing out of nowhere.

Siobhan put the car in gear and was watching for a gap in the passing ranks to insert us into.

But a lone figure came racing towards us on the shoulder, a coyote at a dead run, her ears back. The car behind her flashed its headlights, letting her know it had seen her and that they wouldn't run her over.

I opened the car door, letting the cool night air whoosh in, and the coyote began to shift. In three steps, Aline was back in human form and came leaping in and slammed the door behind her.

I stared at the tanks still coming through the portal.

"Keira came," Aline explained. "She told me to run on ahead." She was white as a sheet.

"That," said Corban, "was awesome. You guys are getting an army through a portal in less than half an hour. Respect, girl."

"That," she replied, "was me getting disowned by my kind forever."

"Except for Keira," I said.

The look she gave me was unreadable. All I could tell from it was that I shouldn't press the issue.

Amy and Gina both leaned forward to squeeze her shoulder and express their gratitude, which seemed to calm her some.

Siobhan pulled the SUV back onto the road and we were once again zooming along with an escort of tanks.

"Thank you," I said to Aline. "Seriously."

"Sooo, just out of curiosity," said Corban, "what was Tobias talking about when he said you had too many ties to humanity?"

The girl ducked her head.

"No," I said, "don't interrogate her about that." Not only was it not fair to Aline, but Amy also had a boyfriend here on Earth who she couldn't reach or help. She'd gotten so stoic in the last few years that she barely ever talked about him, and now wasn't the time to open that can of worms.

Aline looked sidelong at me. "Someone's gotta get you through the portal to the demon realm. Saving the world trumps saving just the people I love."

"Where is he?" Amy asked.

She'd figured it out.

"California," said Aline. "LA. They got hit with a tsunami— the city did, and the San Andreas fault line had a massive earthquake. And..." She looked up ahead. "Something's wrong."

Sure enough, all of the cars in the motorcade were coming to a stop.

TWELVE

"Now," I told Aline. "You have to go. I'm betting this is your kind."

"Agreed," said Siobhan. "You need to protect yourself."

Aline looked around at the rest of us. "I'll be back when I can."

We all nodded and in the blink of an eye, she was gone.

"I do not get how she does that," said Corban. "Without even taking a step, she's gone."

Siobhan flashed her headlights so that other cars would clear a path, allowing her to pull her vehicle off to the side.

I unbuckled my seatbelt.

"Wait," said Corban.

But I opened my car door and jumped out, even as Mouse yelled, "Liana!"

Both she and Corban clambered out after me.

The air was even more chill now that I was all the way outside. I zipped up my jacket as my cheeks began to sting a little. It felt so good to be under a real sky again, one with stars and depths and that didn't feel like a painted dome.

"People can handle whatever it is up at the gate," Mouse insisted.

I paused and turned to face her and Corban. "There have been angels falling on Earth for days now. A big portion of the order has already turned. Are we sure they can handle it? Otuo seemed solid until the moment he wasn't."

By now Siobhan had also exited the SUV, after admonishing my friends to stay inside.

"Okay," said Corban, "I actually have to agree on this point. You caught me in an unnecessary lie how many hours ago?" He turned to Mouse and Siobhan. "One of you come with us, but don't veil us unless you have to. We'll just look to see what's happening."

The two angels exchanged a look.

"I go," said Mouse.

Siobhan nodded and went back into the SUV.

I started to hike towards the rank upon rank of alligator-like tanks that were all at a standstill. This, I realized, was going to be a very long walk.

One of the soldiers from a nearby tank hollered to me and pointed to some of his fellow soldiers unloading what looked like a scooter, except it was big enough to seat the three of us, one in front and two in the back.

"Nice!" said Corban.

Only, Mouse grabbed his shoulder with a grip like iron. "I drive."

"But—"

"I have never driven a motorcycle or scooter, you will not rob me of the chance now." Something about her West African accent and the way she rolled her r's made the statement sound even more solemn, and thus ironic, to my ears. I stifled a giggle.

Corban was unnerved enough to wave her on. "Never?" he muttered. "What was stopping you?"

We climbed in, thanking the soldiers profusely as we did, and buckled our seatbelts. They handed us helmets that were articulated, much like the tanks, and were thus adjustable to fit any head. I paused to prod at mine, marveling at how it could stretch a little, but if I hit it from the outside, the pieces would lock and provide protection.

"Eh," said one of the soldiers. He waggled his finger and said something that I was sure meant, "Don't do that."

I apologized and put it on.

Mouse, who was watching over her shoulder, gave me a brusque nod, and then gunned the engine, which turned out to be electric—quiet and able to accelerate fast. Wind screamed in my ears as we took off and my cheeks went from stinging to burning. Tears leaked out the corners of my eyes as we went tearing through the ranks of the military vehicles and on up to the sandstone gates of the park.

The gate didn't explain why we'd stopped, though. Angels could open any locked door, no matter how it was locked.

No, the only things that could have stopped them would have been fallen angels or coyote-shifters in search of their wayward member. Those were the two groups who could see and track angels.

I just had to make sure that whoever was dealing with whatever blocked us didn't try anything duplicitous or...

We cleared the last rank of military vehicles and I got a clear view of the scene at the gate. The man who stood there, face pale, his gun aimed at the face of the angel speaking to him, was no coyote-shifter. He had normal skin and hair coloring (fair skin and brown hair) and a fear in his eyes that indicated that he had no idea what was going on. The floodlights seemed pale and weak in the otherwise vast darkness of the desert, but I still had to squint a little as we drew near.

The angel speaking to him wore a hijab and spoke what I assumed was Arabic.

"Translate?" I asked Corban.

"Hafsa's saying that he's probably stressed and should relax."

"He can see angels," I said. He was like me.

Hafsa's words were technically true, but only technically. I unbuckled my seatbelt and vaulted out of the scooter. Mouse cursed and followed me, which I thought was a futile gesture, but when we approached the scene, the man didn't turn towards us.

Mouse was a better stealth-er than most. She thought it was strange that I could see her, and now I had some idea why. She was veiling me, too, even though I wasn't trying to be quiet.

Hafsa ignored us.

"Excuse me," I said.

The man swung around, aiming the gun at my head. The fact that I was a young woman didn't make him flinch—he had been pointing a gun at Hafsa's head only a moment before, so I should have expected that.

I definitely did not expect the paralyzing fear I felt at having a gun pointed at me, though. This had never, ever happened to me in my life. Having a vampire's fangs in my neck was nothing compared to this; at least vampires lulled the victims with sex appeal. This was explosive death at the twitch of a finger staring me full in the face, and a pair of wide eyes broadcasting terror from beyond the muzzle of the gun.

I put my hands up. "I'll tell you the truth," I said. "Hafsa's not lying, but I will tell you the full truth." I made a judgment call and looked him in the eye. Normally that was considered flirtation in this part of the world, but these weren't sexy circumstances.

He flinched. He wasn't a very old man, perhaps in his thirties if that. A scruffy beard struggled to establish itself on his chin and jawline, and his Adam's apple bobbed once, twice, as he processed what I said. I did not doubt that he understood me. While the night guards at Petra wouldn't have to know English, I supposed, most of the staff working at Petra did. A lot of people in Jordan did.

The fear in his eyes wasn't pure bewilderment. He was processing my words.

"I will tell you," I said, "and you will think I'm crazy, but I'm telling the truth. Please put the gun down."

"Liana," said Hafsa.

But Corban, who had followed us, shook his head. "Let her. We have to be honest now more than ever; too many of us haven't held the line and look at the price we've paid. All the time we've kept covenants? It was training for split second decisions in times like this."

"Please," I begged the guard. "Put the gun down. You see us, when none of the other guards do?"

I hazarded a guess that there were other guards. I didn't think one of the most famous sites in the world was guarded by a lone guy.

"You're not crazy," I said. "You're exceptional. You're... perceptive. You see things that other people don't. You're good at discerning truth." My hands were starting to tremble, I'd held them up so long. Or perhaps they'd been doing that all along and I only now had the presence of mind to feel it.

Slowly, he lowered the gun. That eye of death at the mouth of the barrel dropped to my throat, chest, stomach, and finally the ground. I went almost boneless with relief. "Thank you."

"Who are you?" he demanded.

"My name's Liana."

"Are you human?"

"Yes," I said, "and no. It's a long story."

"And who are they?" He pointed at the rest of the force assembled.

"The armies of heaven," I said. "Or we're trying to be. We're trying to stop what's happening to the world."

"Abdul!" shouted a voice from the guard house, followed by a string of Arabic.

Corban reacted at once. "No!"

Hafsa burst into near tears and began begging Abdul for something, imploring him.

I looked at Corban, who looked back at me and said, "They say they just called for help, saying he was seeing things."

As if on cue, a peal of thunder sounded in the distance. The fallen had overheard the call. Why did they have to be so efficient with their surveillance?

Abdul looked at me.

"Don't use the phone or radio again," I told him. "The armies of hell are listening, and now they're on their way."

THIRTEEN

ightning came crashing down on all sides. "They're here!" I shouted to Abdul. "Come here into the SUV. It's safer than the guard house! Call your friends!"

Corban dragged me back towards the lead SUV; one of the ones that we'd stolen from Melanie. The soldiers inside climbed out while a coterie of angels poured out of nearby cars and took up defensive positions.

Abdul gave me a look of abject terror, then began yelling at the other guards in Arabic.

They shook their heads. They could hear and see the lightning, but they still couldn't see the huge convoy.

Hafsa raised her arms and shouted. "Come to us for protection!"

And the rest of the angels that had just poured out of their car repeated her cry.

The scales fell from the eyes of the other guards and they looked at the first rank of military vehicles. Their minds would have devised a non-threatening explanation for the sudden appearance.

Corban had dragged me almost to the SUV.

"Come on!" I shouted back to the guards. "In here!"

But they had all raised their guns and were jogging to join the ranks of the military.

More lightning crashed down around us, and the angels up and down the convoy returned fire, shooting ferrum tipped arrows from crossbows.

I hoped, desperately, that Amy and Gina were safe. I should have told them to go with Aline, but there wasn't time to think straight anymore.

Corban all but shoved me into the SUV, screaming at me to get all the way in before he slammed the door, hard enough that my ears rang. The sound of thunder rumbling dampened, but only a little.

I'm in a Faraday cage, I told myself. The science nerd in me was desperate to keep my hind-brain calm, and my hind-brain was screaming that the lightning strikes would electrocute me.

I made myself take some deep breaths and peered out the window at Corban, who was busy shouting orders to the ranks of angels that had formed around my vehicle.

Was that smart? Fallen angels could see regular angels, so was that drawing attention to me?

I turned to look out the back window and saw the soldiers reacting with looks of awe at the horde of angels that had continued to reveal themselves.

The tanks all raised their gun-barrels skyward and began shooting what looked like some kind of electronic pulse, each one punching hard enough that I could feel the recoil as a jolt in the ground.

Boy did I feel like a sitting duck. I did not want to be trapped here.

Lightning punched down, hitting several tanks, which, amazingly, kept on firing. An earthquake caused the ground to shift suddenly to the right, knocking my head against the door of the SUV hard enough that I saw stars.

A figure with lightning wings alighted about ten feet away from my SUV, close enough that I could see that it was a pale skinned woman with blond hair, and the jet black eyes that turned my direction, causing my blood to run cold.

A blur of motion beyond her nearly made my heart stop as a coyote, running full tilt, came bursting out of the rows of tanks and shot towards my car.

Aline, I thought. It had to be.

I opened the car door, letting in the reek of ozone and the sounds of tank fire and thunder as the frightened canine leapt in, bowling me over with sharp claws, bony legs and the reek of wet dog. Corban spun around and shut my door as Mouse launched herself towards the fallen angel.

I turned and found human Aline, her hair still wet, sitting on the floor, curled up into a ball.

"You okay?" I asked.

She looked up at me with red-rimmed eyes and tearstained cheeks and sniffled. "Y-yeah."

"You sure you should be here?"

"I gotta protect you."

An explosion rocked our vehicle on its shocks and I turned to see that one of the tanks had blown up. Shadowy figures—soldiers no doubt—were fleeing in all directions as guardian angels marched into the breach. The fallen angel who'd been staring me down was in hand-to-hand combat with Mouse, and even as they wrestled, forearms locked, another angel slipped around and knifed the fallen in the back, reducing her to dust with what I knew would be a soft popping noise. (One I couldn't hear inside an armored car with explosions happening nearby.)

I let out a breath. That was one down. I marked at least fifty million left, given the frequency of the lightning bolts and the directions they came from. Then again, I was no military strategist. Corban would have a saner number.

Aline pulled herself up onto the seat, wrapping her hair around her hand and pushing it back over her shoulder. Her clothes were wet too, but not as drenched as her hair. Given I didn't understand how she shape-shifted with her clothes anyway, this made about as much sense as I could expect.

"You don't have to protect me," I said. "You should protect yourself."

"If this goes south," she said, "I can take you into the demon realm. I'm afraid that's all I got."

I nodded. "Okay, but the portal's sealed."

"I gave the spell to the Sidhe and I took them over to Petra. They're unsealing it."

"You just did that?" I asked.

"Yeah..." She rubbed her face with her hands. "I just did that and saved who I could and then got back here as fast as I could."

"You saved people, too?" I said. "I'm glad."

"I saved who I could." She blinked, fresh tears slipping down her cheeks. "I couldn't find everyone."

I reached out and pulled her into my arms, giving her the most reassuring hug I could manage.

She burst into tears, her shoulders shaking and her chest convulsing as a bolt of lightning hit the guard-house and blasted down one of the walls, which in turn brought the gate crashing down.

Aline and I ducked as the SUV took the brunt of the impact of falling sandstone bricks which hit with a series of deafening bangs. The ceiling dented and caved in a little, but mostly held. The windows cracked and the driver's side window shattered. Quiet that was loud enough to roar reigned as the dust cleared. After a moment, I could hear the tanks firing and the explosions, but they were muffled now.

Muffled by the huge heap of rubble we were under.

Beyond the cracked windows were just piles of sandstone blocks. The dome light in the SUV came on, some form of emergency system, perhaps? It meant we got a real good look at how trapped we were.

My cellphone rang and Corban's number popped up.

"You're alive?" I answered it.

"You're alive..." He sounded faint with relief.

"The SUV stayed intact," I said. "How did you survive?"

"By running out of the way," he said, a chuckle in his voice. "Okay, so now you're hidden—"

"Corban," I said. "The fallen are monitoring cell phone calls."

"I know but..." He sighed. "Sit tight, okay? We'll dig you out." He didn't ask about Aline and I didn't say anything. There was a chance the fallen hadn't seen her. The line went dead.

She was still tucked under my left arm and I pulled back a little further to get a good look at her. Tearstains reddened her cheeks, but I think the almost-getting-crushed had scared her out of further tears. Her eyes were wide.

"We're okay," I told her.

"I couldn't find Micah."

"If he doesn't know the truth, he's safe," I said. "He can't do anything that'll put a target on his own chest."

But she was crying again.

"Don't waste time imagining the worst," I told her. "Don't obsess about what you can't control, okay? And if you want to go find him—"

"No... I mean I do... but the fate of the world?" She gestured around. "You gotta survive."

"Look if for any reason you don't make it back to him, I'll make sure someone does." It was a crazy promise given I was as likely, if not more likely, to die from this crazy endeavor than she was.

"Th-thanks..."

"I've been in a lot of losing fights," I said. "It's not over until it's over. Okay? Just hang on, here."

"Portal's still sealed," she said. "Any second now they should get it unsealed."

"You translated the spell for them and everything?"

"Oh..." She gave me a wide eyed look.

Uh-oh... I thought.

But then Aline burst out laughing. "Yes. Of course I did."

I gave her a mocking punch in the shoulder. If she could still crack jokes, we just might be all right.

"How's Keira?" I asked.

Aline blinked. "She's dead. They killed her."

"Oh..." I said. "Um... who's they? Your kind?"

She nodded. "I'm the only one left on your side."

FOURTEEN

I cursed my own naïveté. Corban would have known that Keira was dead. One didn't carry out an act of defiance this great without paying the consequences. "She saved you, then."

"Yeah. She... was more human than the others ever were."

"Were?" I asked. How bad was this civil war getting?

"A third of us are dead."

"What?" I tried not to scream the word. "A third of your kind are dead?"

Aline lifted one arm in a shrug. "There are only twelve of us at any given time."

"Oh..." Well, that explained why they didn't bother with having rules or a hierarchy. They all knew each other. "And four are dead?"

"Everyone but Tobias and the babies."

"Babies?" I asked.

"Yeah, we'd already gotten all the little ones into a safe house, and I moved them," she explained. "Now I know where they are and Tobias doesn't and the mundane guardians aren't gonna tell him because they hate him and like me."

"It pays to be nice to people," I agreed. "Aline, I had no idea. Seriously, this is more than anyone should deal with ever."

She shrugged again. It wasn't a dismissive gesture. It was an expression that she had no alternatives.

"I lost my dad when I was near your age," I said. "I thought I lost my universe. This is worse."

"That's still pretty bad."

"This is worse," I repeated.

Aline nodded, a tear leaking down her cheek. Before I could hug her again, though, she dove for the glove compartment in the front seat and pawed through it, coming up with some scraps of paper. With a pen dug out of her pocket, she began writing something down. "Micah's phone number, and name and stuff," she said. "And the phone number to reach the mundanes raising the babies."

I nodded. "Okay, let me write some stuff down for you." I took a piece of paper and wrote down my lawyer's number and the address and location of the spare key for Aunt Cassie's off-grid home in Taos. Then I put the numbers that Aline had given me into my phone, so that I would have two copies, one there and one hardcopy that I slipped in my pocket. Then I texted my lawyer.

"What's your full name?" I asked her.

"Aline... um... Hulsman."

The boyfriend's name. Well, husband's. I nodded and tapped out a message telling my lawyer to look out for an Aline Hulsman if she ever came to him needing anything. I also listed Corban, Siobhan, and my best friends in the text. I also had to remember to tell my lawyer who I was, since this wasn't my phone. Then I shut off the phone. I didn't know how long it would be before I could recharge it, so I needed to save its battery.

I tried not to focus on what a puny, last ditch effort this was to look out for the people we loved. "So, I heard about Denise," I said.

"Tobias exiled her."

"I'm sorry."

"And I don't know where. She's somewhere in the universe, and I have no idea where."

"I am really, really sorry."

Aline fisted tears out of her eyes. "He's the one who's going to be sorry."

I hoped that was true, and that Aline wouldn't have to be the one to make him so.

There came the sound of a loud bang, like metal striking stone.

Aline's eyes widened and her body went rigid. "What's that?"

"That," I said, "sounds like someone commandeered one of the tanks and is coming after us." That was inevitable after Corban's call. I knew the forces would have protected us as best they could without giving away our location and importance, but any measures to hold them off would be temporary.

"The portal still isn't open," said Aline, as another metallic strike rang out. "It should be by now. It's a short spell."

I could see her start to spin-out as her mind grappled with likely scenarios. Not good. "Hey," I said, "is there anything you can do to get us away from here?"

She looked at me, eyes dilated. "From right here?"

"Yeah."

She blinked. "I can take you to the nether-realm and right back. We-we can't stay there. We can't travel around in there. I can get us to over there." She pointed towards the front seats, meaning beyond the gates and inside the park, I assumed. "But it won't be far. Like, fifteen feet from the edge of the collapsed gate? Maybe more. I don't know how far the rubble spread. We'll be completely exposed, though."

"Well, here we're dead," I pointed out as the blows picked up speed. The ceiling of the SUV creaked ominously. "I think they're just looking to crush us."

Aline nodded. "Okay."

"And if you can get yourself away, do that," I told her.

She shot me another unreadable look, took me by the shoulder, and pulled me forward out of my seat.

We both landed on our hands and knees on the flat plain of the nether-world, which had gone dim. That was probably coincidence, but it felt ominous.

A whirring noise made me look up. I startled and fell back as I saw what looked like alien, mechanical jellyfish flying through the air towards us.

"Wh-what are—" I began.

"Move," shouted Aline, yanking my arm so that we broke into a run.

When we portalled again, I braced myself for pouring rain, lightning, laser fire, even fallen angels bearing right down on us. What I got instead was silence—not even my footfalls made a sound. It felt like I was running on pavement and I slowed my steps, looking around.

"Aline?" I said. I kept my voice soft. If anyone overheard us, that could be the end of her.

The darkness around me resolved into a sky ablaze with stars, complete with the cloudy line of the Milky Way arcing straight overhead.

I blinked. Where were the tall plateaus and other land features of the Jordanian desert? Where was the rain? Where was the war? Where was everyone else?

I turned a slow, full circle and tried to get my bearings. Behind me was a great stone arch that glowed softly. A free-standing parabola; imposing because it stood alone. It was probably only about thirty feet high at its keystone, but in this strangeness it loomed higher than the St. Louis Gateway to the West.

The stars, now that I looked at them, were all wrong. I couldn't place any constellations. Not the Big Dipper or Orion's Belt. Not the Little Dipper or the W-shape of Casseopeia. The Milky Way wasn't even in the right part of the sky. I couldn't, off the top of my head, say where it ought to be, but I knew that it was at the wrong height, and it was thicker that I'd ever seen it, even high in the pollution free mountains of Earth.

I wasn't on Earth. I was standing on a high platform in some other place, some other realm, and Aline hadn't come with me.

I'd made it to the demon realm.

Someone cleared their throat behind me and I spun around so fast that I almost fell over. There, standing a few feet away, was me. Or... almost me. She looked like my vampire self with her perfectly slim body, lustrous hair, and fair skin, except hers was pale as death. She glowed slightly, with a luminosity that went beyond the paleness of her skin. Her whole being glowed like an eighties Hollywood effect, like something from one of the Tron movies. It washed her out, slightly, making her look ethereal.

The other difference was her eyes. They weren't the brown eyes I'd seen in the mirror every day of my life. They were pitch black, like those of a fallen angel.

"Liana," she said.

I put my hands up. "Who are you?"

"Oh, you've only had me with you for how many years?" she taunted.

I looked down at myself and saw, for the first time in years, my normal body. My belly slouched; my thighs weren't straight.

My mind scrabbled to make sense of this situation.

She's my demon. The demon who'd tried to possess my body and turn me into a vampire was free now.

Was my job really as simple as getting all the demon carriers through the portal so that their demons could be set free? Would this return these creatures back to their own realm so that the portal would collapse and our worlds could part ways without whatever carnage awaited Earth?

No... I realized. Otuo had stayed a guardian angel after returning to Earth. Gamlat had become a vampire. If I left this realm, this demon would come with me.

Which meant she probably wasn't going to let me leave this realm.

"I'm glad you're free now," I said.

Her smile wasn't one of joy or happiness, or even relief. It was of pure cruelty. "Am I free?"

"Interesting choice of words," said another voice. Corban's voice.

Only the man who stepped through the arch wasn't Corban. He looked like him, but also had the glow and the pitch black eyes, and his smile was also pure cruelty.

"I... I mean you no harm," I said.

"Oh but you do," said my demon. "Our only saving grace is that you have no idea what you're doing. And we are not going to let you figure it out." And with that, she and the Corban-demon came at me.

Part 2:

Corban

FIFTEEN

ouse and I were fighting, back-to-back, daggers up, ready to repel any of the fallen who came for us. They weren't interested in two measly little individuals like us, though.

Rain poured down, plastering my hair to my head and my clothes to my body. Mouse's back was chill against mine and my heart was pounding, but I forced myself to ignore that and focus on what was going on. My military training allowed me to see past the fighting and pick out the patterns of how people moved and where the enemy was pressing in.

There were two fallen left.

I hated feeling so useless as lightning bolts rained down and shadowy figures with lightning wings shot past overhead.

Off to my left, Hafsa was standing still, face calm, glare focused on me. The one skill I retained from being an angel was the ability to see my own kind.

Her stillness, that wasn't a good sign. I'd kept my eye on her because Liana had flagged her as skating too close to the edge.

Her eyes were darkening, and in a moment a massive bolt of lightning would strike, announcing to the universe that another angel had turned all the way.

I tapped Mouse on the arm and then made a beeline through the pouring rain for Hafsa. "Hold it together!" I shouted at her. "Stay strong. You can do this."

The look she gave me wasn't fearful or nervous. It was contemptuous.

"I'll cover you," shouted Mouse.

I pelted the last few feet until I was toe-to-toe with my angelic sister. How was it that Liana could pick out our weakest members unfailingly? A stopped motorcade had been all she needed to figure out Hafsa wasn't as strong as she needed to be.

I grabbed her by the arms and she jerked away. Appropriate, given her mortal culture, but not for an angel. We touched people all the time to let them know that they weren't alone. Her attention came fully to me and she curled her lips in a cruel smile. Blackness flooded through her eyes and sparks flew from her fingertips.

With practiced precision from slaying vampires, I slipped my dagger between her ribs and into her heart. Her eyes only widened slightly before she popped out of existence, collapsing in a small pile of muddy ash that began to wash away in rivulets even as I watched.

Several others of my kind ran at me, which made sense. I'd gone after one of our own. This was why Mouse had been so careful to cover me. She stood with one hand upraised.

"She was turning," I said. "I swear it." I had to shout to be heard over the laser fire and the sound of a tank exploding in the distance.

Just then another tank broke ranks and headed for us.

Now, that was not the action of someone on our side.

"Fallen!" I shouted.

Mouse loosed a crossbolt at a shadowy figure hovering just above. Her aim was flawless and the dark rain that poured down was water mixed with ash.

That meant the last attacker was in that tank, which was headed for the pile of sandstone blocks that had been the front gates of the park. With a rearing back, the tank brought its front claws down on the rubble. Its goal was plain: to smash whatever was underneath flat as a pancake and kill whoever was inside.

The SUVs could take a lot, I knew, but I wasn't sure how bad of a beating this one had taken when the gate collapsed on it. It was best to assume that it was about to buckle all the way.

I held up my hands and shouted, "Make way!"

I ran towards the tank only to have Mouse tackle me from behind. One moment I was running, the next I was down, my shoulder and back striking the pavement as we rolled. She got to her feet faster than I did and before I could recover myself, she'd disappeared into the dark night.

But Siobhan was now standing over me with her palm out, motioning for me to stay down. "Don't try to be the hero," she shouted. "You're not built for it anymore."

This was true. Mouse was impervious to all but ferrum projectiles, which were only possessed by our side. That meant she could go barreling through the thick of battle without dying.

I caught the flicker of a shadow crossing near the hatch of the tank, and then the entire thing shuddered to a stop. Soldiers gathered around, weapons at the ready to fire if the wrong kind of being emerged from the hatch.

The hatch popped open and no one reacted.

I relaxed. That was Mouse, then.

The rain still slapped down creating a dull roar of noise, but it was the only noise left. No more shots fired, no more lightning bolts coming down.

I tipped my head forward and took some deep breaths, choking on the rainwater. "We did it," I said. "We did it!"

Muffled cheers sounded all around—muffled in part by the weather, which was at least starting to slacken, and muffled in part by the dampening force of things not going exactly how we'd have liked. A massive battle at the gates to Petra had not been in the plan.

But the tanks behind me were pulling back into their formation and the soldiers were all wiping their brows as the rain began to slacken.

I scanned the crowd for Abdul, the poor guard at the gate who'd gotten so much more than he'd bargained for tonight.

Through the dwindling rain, I caught sight of him clasping forearms with one of the field commanders.

He was alive. Good.

I headed over towards them. "Are your friends alive?" I asked, in Arabic.

He turned, blinked, then nodded. "Where is the girl who was with you?"

I pointed at the pile of rubble that was the gate. "The car survived underneath that."

He still gave me a startled look.

One of the tanks was maneuvering to shift blocks of sandstone aside. Now that it wasn't a life or death situation, I didn't dare call her.

The tank had a gripping, clawlike appendage that was able to move the rocks—these were some seriously advanced vehicles. It made me wonder how many realms were ahead of Earth technologically.

Shouts to my left caught my attention as a bedraggled dog came bolting though the crowd.

No, not a dog. Too skinny and lithe. It was a coyote with its ears back and its gaze darting everywhere. I couldn't say for sure how I knew it was Aline, but I knew, and I moved to block her as she went to dart past me.

With a startled jerk of her head, she saw me, and then the coyote was gone and the girl came skidding to a stop, eyes wide and startled.

"What's wrong?" I asked.

"I can't find her."

"Can't find who?" I knew the answer before I finished the sentence, and my heart felt like it was being ripped in half.

"Liana. I portalled her out of the car when they started bashing on us, and I tried to portal us back, but she's not there and she's not here."

"Tried to portal her to where?" I asked. My shoulders were going tense, though. Liana was tough and resourceful, but not invisible.

"J-just the nether-realm and back. Just to move us a few feet, out of the car. B-but when we came back, she didn't come with me. I don't know what happened or how or—"

"She's not stuck in the portal?" I asked.

"The nether-realm is in the portal. You get stuck in a portal, you're stuck in the nether-realm."

"Oh, right." I pretended to understand that.

"Sh-she's not there. I swear. I've looked and I've come back here and I've looked all around..."

I put my hands on her shoulders. "Okay, relax. We'll find her." I was speaking to myself as much as her. Panicking right now wouldn't help the situation.

"She can't stay in the nether-realm, though. I-I tried to make it safer in case she is stuck there, but she can't be there for much longer."

"Why not?"

By now the rain had lifted and the night was clearing up. One of the soldiers passed by, handing out mylar blankets. I grabbed one eagerly—my drenched clothing and the freezing cold were not a good mix.

I pressed another mylar blanket into Aline's hands, but her clothing was merely damp, not soaking wet. Cold wasn't what was making her hands shake.

"Because if my kind find her, they're gonna kill her," she said. "He's going to kill her."

"Who is?" I demanded.

"Tobias. Tiger stripes. Who else? He hates you guys and he knows I'm on your side. He's totally going to try to kill you all."

SIXTEEN

Do. Not. Panic, I told myself.

The advantage of being with a couple of military units was that it was easy to organize people into search parties to sweep the area around the collapsed gate. Another tank was tasked with lifting aside more rubble, just in case Liana had materialized under it.

Though Aline assured us that things didn't work that way. People couldn't materialize inside of solid objects any more than they could walk through them while they weren't portalling.

A small team of us went with Aline over to the nether-realm, where it wasn't exactly warm, but it was less cold than the Jordanian night. It was dark here, too, though the sky glowed with a pale version of what might have been moonlight. The hospital was easy to spot on the horizon, but otherwise the land was so empty it might as well have been a dead world. I felt like a lame, childish dress-up version of a superhero with my mylar blanket around my shoulders.

Siobhan and Mouse, who'd both managed to change to dry clothes, struck out as soon as we arrived, scanning our surroundings for any sign of Liana.

Aline just stood where she'd materialized and began to sob.

Siobhan and Mouse were fighters. I was competent at war, but I had also spent over a dozen centuries counseling young adults, and Aline was both a young adult and the person with the most information about where my beloved was. "Aline," I said, planting myself in front of her. "It's all right."

"You don't know that."

Okay, so she wasn't much for the usual, empty talk that people babbled in stressful situations. I could respect that.

"It will be all right," I modulated. "You were trying to save her. Definitely the right move."

She blinked away some of her tears and looked at me. "I turned off the drones patrolling here, but Tobias will turn them back on when he can."

"Or one of the rest of you will stop him. Keira, for example."

The look Aline gave me was almost pitying.

My blood ran cold. "Then you're in danger," I said.

She shook her head. "There's only Tobias, and he won't move against me. He'll go for Liana."

"Only Tobias?" All I could do was stare. This kid had just survived a genocide? That had been going on during our little skirmish at Petra?

"The rest killed each other," she said. "It was, like, simmering for a long time. Bunch of psychopaths." She hiccuped another sob.

"Aline... How big of a body count are we talking, here?"

"Four are dead. Tobias is going after Liana, and I got all the babies. The little ones. They're safe."

"So... how many of you are there?" I asked. In my mind I tried to recall how many coyote-shifters had been hanging around in the hospital. My memory could pick out five... including Tobias.

"Um, eight are left? Which is a deep secret. Don't go, like, telling it to strangers. Liana knows, though."

"There are only twelve of you?"

"At a time, yeah. But six right now are kids. Babies and little kids." More tears were streaming down her cheeks.

Well, that explained why sightings of her kind were so rare. Digging further into this topic was clearly not what Aline wanted, and I already knew it wasn't what I needed. I changed the subject. "So where's Tobias? Could he have snatched Liana?"

"I doubt it. I told him I'd kill him if he came near me or the babies," said Aline. "He'll believe me. Not that I'm gonna actually kill him. He doesn't know that, though. He doesn't get me. I'm not like the rest of my kind. I'm not insane."

A lot of supernaturals had empathy issues. It came with having powers. Aline was more like Liana and angels who stayed stable. She had an extra measure of human compassion.

Siobhan and Mouse had finished ranging over the immediate area and were jogging back to us. "She's not here, Corban!"

Siobhan called out. "And Aline wouldn't have missed her if she was. This place is so flat."

"I assume you went coyote and ran around a bit in here?" asked Mouse.

Aline nodded.

"And were you able to pick up her trail? With your coyote nose?" asked Siobhan.

"Yeah, I was. It's really short. Ends there." She pointed to a spot on the ground about six feet away.

Mouse gave Aline a sympathetic pat on the arm. "You didn't lose her, did you? Something happened. Explain what happened."

"No, we know what happened," said Siobhan. "On Earth, it was pouring rain, more people, no scent trail. She's over there, all right? It'll be okay."

But Aline shook her head. "She didn't come through over there. I mean, I get it. That's where she has to be, but she wasn't with me when I came through."

"Fine," said Mouse, her dark figure little more than a shadow in the dimness with the whites of her eyes picking up a little stray light. "So what does that mean? You've portalled how many times? You tell us how this works."

"It um... it means that she portalled somewhere else. Like if you're walking down a path and they turn down another branch. But, like, okay... she can't portal on her own. If she was one of my kind, yeah. But she's a mundane."

I reminded myself that when one was as powerful as a coyote-shifter, everyone who couldn't portal at will was a "mundane." Even a vampire.

"People can cross realms when they're destined to," Siobhan pointed out.

"The demon realm is sealed," said Aline. "Or... it was..." She scrunched her face. "Hang on." She began to walk.

"Whoa—" I said, catching her arm. "If there are only two adult coyote-shifters left and the other one is evil, do not leave us in the nether-realm. Please. If anything happens to you..."

"Oh, right." She motioned for us to follow her.

Mouse and Siobhan both gave me shocked looks.

A few steps and we were back by the gate to Petra, on the side inside the park. The cold, damp air was a shock to my system, but the SUV with my gear in it was parked only a few feet away.

Thank the Lord for small blessings. I ran to it, rummaged in the back, and put on a dry shirt and trousers, dumping the wet ones over the back bumper.

"Um..." said Gina, leaning over the back of the seat. "Can we get out now?"

I jumped in surprise. Not that I worried about her ogling me or anything. I just felt stupid for forgetting she was there.

"There's a rogue coyote shifter on the loose and Liana's missing," I said. Because I had to, because it was the truth.

"Wait, what?" said Amy, poking her head up to stare at me, too.

"I know, I know. We're trying to find her, but you guys... please stay in the bulletproof vehicle. If you can duck down, that would be ideal."

"Liana—" Gina began.

"Is probably safe. I'm on it. Aline's on it."

"A rogue shifter took her?" asked Amy.

"No, no. I'm guessing she's in the demon realm. Seriously, stay here, please. Get some sleep if you can."

"Would you be able to?" Gina asked.

"No."

"Fine, we'll try," said Amy. "They may need us later, we can't portal anywhere now, on our own," she said to Gina.

The two obediently lay down.

I hoisted my backpack out and put it on before shutting the back doors.

Beyond the SUV, there was a steady stream of soldiers picking their way through a cleared path in the wreckage of the gateway. I didn't see Abdul anywhere, but assumed he was fine with this. We'd won against the fallen. Surely that was sufficient to show we were the good guys?

Aline stood with my other two friends a few feet away with her head up and her chin lifted. Slowly she shook her head. "There's something going on with the portal." She began to jog towards it.

I resolved to catch up with her and Mouse and Siobhan. "If it's anything bad or potentially violent," I said, "you let us handle it, all right? You stay back."

She shot me a baffled look.

"If there's seriously only one of you left on our side," said Siobhan, "then yes, we treat you like you're the queen of the universe."

"Pampered and not allowed to do anything," Mouse chimed in.

Aline looked back at us, then shrugged. "I dunno if it's bad or violent or what."

"Well, do you think Tobias would intervene at the portal in any way?" I asked.

"Why bother?" she replied. "He doesn't care, is the thing. He doesn't want to expend effort to help with the fight against realms tearing apart. I don't see why he'd do anything to hinder the fight, either."

"What does he care about?" I asked.

"Nothing much."

"Everyone cares about something," I said. "Think about it and let me know."

She shook her head. "He wants me to be... available to him."

I thought this over as quickly as I could. "Your kind don't typically date mundanes?"

"Right."

So if there were only a few of them, then their romantic options were limited. I might have been fully committed to Liana, but I wasn't blind. Aline was cute. "He likes you."

"No," Aline fired back, "he feels entitled to me. Not the same thing."

"Fair point."

"And he's twenty-six."

"Yeah, no," said Siobhan. "Not in this era. Not in your culture. Hard 'no' on that one."

I picked up the pace, grateful that I'd spent a lot of time working out. "We gotta get to the portal," I said. "If he feels entitled to you, he is likely to pull something here."

"But—"

"He knows this is what you care about. If he can't have you, he's going to mess with you," I said. "Trust me, I've seen thousands of abusers. Millions. Entitled men? Not a new phenomenon in this world, I'm afraid."

"Who's at the portal?" Siobhan wanted to know.

"The Sidhe," said Aline.

"How many of them?" I asked. Since their heyday, the Sidhe's population had fallen. They were only a few hundred strong anymore.

"Um... like a lot?"

I picked up the pace. "We've gotta get there now!"

SEVENTEEN

I ended up tossing my backpack aside and breaking into the fastest run I could. My gear was not a priority right now. The vehicles were still not able to drive into the park—too much rubble in the way—so we had to hot-foot it.

Mouse and Siobhan kept up and a few moments later, a coyote joined our all out, pelting dash.

We were following the road for tourists that ran from the gates into the canyon where the treasury was. This was a famous ruin, the outside of which had been used in Indiana Jones and the Last Crusade as the location of the Holy Grail because it was an impressive looking edifice. Carved right into the side of the canyon, into the raw cliff face, was its ornate, columned entrance that stretched several stories up.

It was Amy who had noted that the outside had been worked extensively and the inside barely at all, and from this she'd made the leap to figuring out that it was a portal. What was on the inside was secondary because when used for its real purpose, people didn't go through the door and end up inside the treasury. Nabatean edifices like their treasury weren't all portals, but this one definitely was.

And so I was relieved when we entered the canyon and saw the cliffs rising high on either side of us. The trickle of people moving in thinned out as a lot of them were tired from the battle and probably not in the mood for a march right now. There weren't too many angels in the group or...

I couldn't help it. I slowed my steps.

Siobhan and Mouse were visible to me, but I knew they were there and so did Aline. They weren't veiled at the moment.

"What is it?" Siobhan asked as I processed this.

"Aline!" I called out.

The coyote, who had run on ahead, stopped and turned, ears forward. She came jogging back towards us, shifting into human form as she did—casually showing who knew how many soldiers and angels what she was.

She came to a stop in front of me, waiting.

"Am I still a demon carrier?" I asked.

"Your threads are really light."

"Look close. Are they there at all?"

She blinked, then squinted, then leaned in so close that it was borderline uncomfortable. Then she reared back.

"I'm not, am I?"

Siobhan and Mouse exchanged a look. "Corban," said Siobhan. "What are you on about?"

I looked down at myself. My body was still fit—but I'd kept it that way over my long life. I suspected my face had changed, though. My eyes wouldn't be ethereal blue, and my hair wouldn't style itself anymore.

"My demon is gone. I'm fully human now."

Aline bit her lip. "Like, I have never heard of that happening before. I swear."

I looked at the stream of people walking past. The angels would be invisible to me now.

"It doesn't seem to be happening to anyone else," Aline assured me.

Shouts rang out from up ahead and I cursed myself for stopping over my own lack of a demon. Big picture, I told myself as I broke into a run.

Aline sprang forward, shifting as she did, and took off way faster than I, on my two legs, could go.

"Aline!" I shouted. "Wait up." I put my head down and pounded the pavement as hard as I could with my feet, not bothering to conserve any energy for the fight once I got there. That was what adrenaline was for.

Both Siobhan and Mouse were faster, too—I told myself it was because they were still supernatural, even though that probably wasn't the reason. Mouse had been able to outrun and outfight me even when she'd been a mortal and I an angel.

Aline was disappearing around the bend and I put on a fresh burst of speed, heedless of the stitch forming in my side.

Soldiers had turned and were running back the way they'd come. One of them shouted a word that might have been, "Fight!" in a French derived language.

Reading as much as I could from the situation, I took that to mean a fight they either felt unprepared for, or felt shouldn't involve them. I prayed for the latter, because I was no more prepared than they were, and still I sprinted on.

The treasury drew into view on the left and I saw then that there was nobody standing outside of it. Even as I watched, Siobhan approached the entrance and jerked forward, as if punched in the back.

"Get down!" I shouted with the last of my breath. There weren't a ton of places to take cover; the ground in front of the treasury was pretty flat and open, but some of the soldiers had discarded their packs and I grabbed one to use as a shield.

Aline, in coyote form, appeared in the doorway.

"Get!" I shouted. "Go! Aline! Get away!"

She ducked aside just as something pocked the frame of the doorway.

Great, so we were in some sort of firefight that was damaging ancient, world heritage sites. Because that was a good use of time, while the world was ending.

A blur of movement was another coyote running from behind a small stack of discarded packs towards the treasury.

Well, if he was running and in coyote form, he wasn't shooting. I went for him, leaping over the pack I'd ducked behind and aiming for well ahead of him. He was running fast, so I had to take that into consideration to intercept him

But he was too fast. He flashed through the door before I could make a skidding turn and follow him.

"Corban, down!" Aline shouted.

She said it fast enough and forcefully enough that I reacted on instinct and flattened myself on the ground just as a great blinding light switched on.

As I lay there, blinking and squinting, the scene resolved itself into Aline holding a flashlight aloft like the Columbia Studios logo before a film. Everyone else was down as well, save for a coyote standing right in front of me, Mouse, and Siobhan— who could not be harmed by bullets.

Tobias was lashing his tail slowly, tauntingly, and he looked right at Aline.

"I will kill you," she said.

For the sake of selling it, I began to scrabble to one side, since I was directly behind him and thus in the theoretical line of fire.

My pulse was stabilizing though, and my senses were sharpening a little more as a result. This was when I noticed that the air reeked of blood.

Another glance around at the prone figures showed me why. They'd been killed, all of the Sidhe who'd come to open the portal. From virtual strangers to Liana's former roommate, they'd each been shot in the head.

They said hell hath no fury like a woman scorned—a needless and absurd sexism. Men didn't handle being scorned very well, and were actually, in my experience, more likely to do things like this. Selfish, awful atrocities to hurt whoever had the audacity to tell them "no."

I wished I had a gun. Ferrum weapons were what worked on fallen angels, and ferrum worked best in dagger and arrowhead form (and I was no archer). I could throw my dagger, but I wasn't practiced at killing animals this way.

I flicked my wrist, moving my dagger from its sheath and into my hand as Tobias went from being a silhouette to a lit figure, thanks to my moving around to one side of him. His laughing eyes didn't change as he began to shift.

Okay, okay, I thought. He was becoming a target I could take out.

Aline was pale as a sheet, hands shaking, on the verge of dropping the flashlight. She reached behind her.

That was okay. I had this. I squeezed the hilt of my dagger, reminding myself of its weight and balance as I readied a throw.

Tobias, the tiger-stripe-haired shifter, came into full human form, a bitter smirk on his face. Then, with a pop and a jerk, the light went out of his eyes.

In shock, I watched him collapse to the floor, then looked at Aline, who held a gun in one hand. "I told you I'd kill you," she said.

Both Siobhan and Mouse were in shock, too. They looked over at me, startled; then we all stared at Aline, who dropped the gun, her face still white, tears running down her cheeks.

I scrabbled to my feet. "Hey," I said. "It's all right. You did what you had to do."

"Bloody hell," said Siobhan. "That was quite a shot, girl."

Mouse slipped over to Tobias's crumpled form and checked for signs of life. "You got him," she said. "Well done."

More tears flowed down Aline's cheeks as she crumpled to the ground.

I felt for her, but I also needed to get to Liana. It took all of my self-control not to go over and shake the girl, demanding she get us to the demon realm.

EIGHTEEN

I made myself be a gentleman and helped Aline sit up and lean against the wall. Siobhan had gone to speak to the troops while Mouse was dragging the bodies of the Sidhe outside. I caught a glimpse of Cecily's body.

What a complete waste.

Aline, to her credit, was getting herself under control. "I told him I'd kill him," she kept muttering. "I told him."

"You did," I said, "and that's war. He just killed our last chance to get the portal open." I hoped and prayed she'd contradict me.

"Someone opened it, but it's closed again."

"What do you mean, someone opened it?" I asked.

"It opened for, like, a split second when I was portalling Liana around, and it's closed again. Like, if the spell gets interrupted, that happens. It doesn't open all the way and stay open."

"And because you were portalling at the time..."

"Liana could have crossed into the demon realm because she's destined to go there, yeah."

All of our plans of sending in a scouting party first, then the military, those were out the window.

No, I told myself. I'd lived long enough to know better than to lose my head. I needed to plan how to help Liana out. If she was in the demon realm, she couldn't die. According to the ancient texts I'd read, no one died there. That didn't mean she couldn't be trapped, tortured, skinned alive... Stop, I told myself.

"How do we get the portal open without the Sidhe? Do we go beg other Sidhe to help? Other communities of them?" I asked.

"Um... I guess we could. Or Fae, or witches, or mages, or wizards."

There were quite a few kinds of magic user in the human race.

Aline swiped at her eyes again with the back of her hand. The light from the flashlight, which we'd set upright on the ground, gave her features a severe, harshly shadowed look. "I can portal some people to the mage enclave in Kansas," she offered. "It's completely safe to go through the nether-realm now."

Now that she said that, I realized the mages in Kansas were the best group to approach. They knew about angels, for one thing, and had worked with us before. They had fought against vampires—and had singlehandedly kept the American MidWest free of them for two hundred years. If anyone would help us, they would.

"Okay," I said. "We'll see about chartering a plane to get them here." Just in case Aline didn't return. Though if she didn't return, none of the rest of us were getting through this portal.

"I'll get them here," said Aline. "And I'll get you guys into the demon realm, and then... I need to try to find Micah. Sorry, I do want to save the world—"

"But the kind of people who save the world," I said, "care about other people." I had no idea who Micah was, but I suspected he was the boyfriend. "You gotta be what you are." This had been proven to me time and again through my lifetime. "We'll get camp set up here. You recover, and then you go get the mages, and as soon as you've done what you can here, go find your guy."

"You don't want to come talk to the mages?" Aline asked.

I shook my head. I had to stay close to the portal. If it opened or Liana came back, I wanted to be here. Also, I wasn't much of a negotiator, and we had angels who were. Every single one who was here knew how important this was. They'd put their lives on the line for it.

Aline nodded. Siobhan and Mouse took over then, shooing me away and telling me to help set up camp. I got stiffly to my feet and headed on out of the treasury, into the night.

There was no scooter, no way to cut this walk short to go get supplies. It was going to be a hike, and how was I going to stop obsessing about Liana and the fate of the world? Despite my advanced age, I'd never lived during a time when I'd been aware that the world needed to be saved nor known the person tasked with it. As a Christian, I believed Christ's life was such a time, and my life had overlapped with his by a few years, but only a few. He'd been crucified when I was still a toddler.

That meant that in my world view, I'd come to adulthood with the great, saving deed already done, with a path to a higher way of living open that I'd merely had to set my foot upon when introduced by Paul the Apostle. When I'd been sentenced to die because my Christian beliefs prevented me from following Roman law, an angel had appeared in my cell and helped me ascend to become an angel myself.

As most understood the story, when the world needed saving, there had been vast supernatural powers in play that had done just that. Now I needed to remember that Christ had been, to most of the people who knew him, a regular guy, a single voice preaching in occupied Israel, telling its people that military and political freedom were beside the point. How pathetic had his message seemed when the Jews were so desperate for their independence?

Having a single woman fighting to stop human civilization from being shredded was a another form of the great war between good and evil. And Liana might be just a girl, but big moments often came down to small people.

She would do this or die trying. Twice she'd faced down powerful vampires, often running straight into the arms of danger in order to prevent others from getting hurt. She'd survived thanks to a mix of her own intelligence, decisiveness, and what I firmly believe was divine providence. What she was doing now was even more important. I had to believe she'd find her way through.

IN THE END, a delegation of five angels went with Aline into the nether-realm and on to Kansas.

I, meanwhile, helped lay out the encampment, and we spent the rest of the night pitching tents, setting up latrines, and breaking the time up into watches. Angels patrolled the area, keeping the encampment hidden. Since the gatehouse had been destroyed, Abdul didn't need to manufacture an excuse for his bosses to consider the park closed.

Besides, it wasn't a great time for tourism on planet Earth. The newsfeed on my cellphone was a steady stream of natural disasters and cities being damaged and destroyed.

It was four in the morning before things were settled and I could retreat into my tent. Mine was pitched inside the treasury. As I zipped the flaps shut, it occurred to me that if the portal opened again and anything came out, I'd be on the front lines.

Demons didn't need the portal to get out, though. They came over even while it was shut, so it was probably not worth worrying about. Nevertheless, I decided to cut my toenails before I went to bed.

Yes it was silly, but it was also a way to activate the spell that protected a dwelling from vampires—just in case the demon realm inhabitants worked according to the rules of vampirism.

I AWOKE TO a scratching on the door of my tent. "Corban?"

Mouse's voice.

"Corban, the Kansas mages are coming."

I rolled over and blinked in the dimness. It wasn't as dark in my tent as it had been when I'd fallen asleep. That meant the sun was up, but I didn't know how high. My warrior-trained internal clock seemed to have fled with my demon. Or perhaps I'd really been pushed beyond what I could handle.

I unzipped the door and found my old friend looking haggard, her skin ashy. Being an angel provided all kinds of support for our mortal bodies, but those bodies still endured wear and tear when we over-exerted ourselves.

"They are coming," she repeated. "Aline is bringing them. She's... she's having a hard time. Personally, that is."

"Right," I croaked. "Well, once she gets us into the demon realm, she can resume her search for the guy she loves. Looks like love, at least." People didn't think teenagers fell in love, and wouldn't it have been convenient if they didn't? The truth was they did. It was one of the great perils of adolescence.

"Yes. Well, the mages sent a written message with a teleportation spell. That's the last we'll hear before they arrive."

"Rest," I ordered her. "I'll—"

"You still need more sleep," she ordered me. "I'll be fine. I just knew you'd want to know about the mages."

"I'm awake now. I'm not going to go back to sleep."

Mouse looked most unimpressed with me. I had no doubt that if she was mortal and keyed up, but knew, intellectually, that she needed sleep, she'd be able to knock herself out cold through sheer will.

The thing was, I had never been the most talented or skillful person I'd ever met, so I didn't mind her disdain. It was a simple fact of my world that I could not do this thing, so I wasn't going to try. I stepped out of the tent.

"Where's the strategy planning going on?" I asked.

She sighed. "Main tent, to the left of the entrance. They have it sorted, already, but if you want to watch them, go ahead."

MOUSE WAS RIGHT, of course. That was a given with her. The various generals were all standing around a 3D projection of the demon realm making plans for how they'd enter. I had nothing to add, so I simply watched as they delineated who would go in first, how they would hold their position, and how they would establish a secure foothold in the demon realm. The demons couldn't be killed, so they would have to be held off.

It wasn't a battle I knew how to fight any better than they did. Nevertheless, I was impressed at their ingenuity, setting up barrier after barrier that they would push outwards as the rest of us poured in. When we went into the demon realm, we'd be building a fortress around ourselves.

I listened until my mind finally grasped the fact that things were as good as they could be, and I really did need more sleep. I stumbled most of the way back to my tent.

SCREAMS, I DON'T know how many hours later, woke me up.

NINETEEN

I bolted to my feet and set my hand on the zipper pull to my tent flap, then hesitated and listened.

The screams were slowly dying down, though the ones that remained were blood curdling, like people having their skin stripped off slowly. Yes, I did know what that sounded like. It'd been far too common in the Middle Ages.

But this all sounded like something else as well, and my still sleep-addled brain was convinced that what I was hearing was a rapid vampire infestation. That used to happen in the Middle Ages too, when large groups of vampires still existed and could come swarming into communities and overwhelm them.

A horde of hungry vampires could level a village in under an hour if people didn't stay in their houses.

This had gone faster.

I had the sense that I was the last man on Earth in that moment, though I hoped and prayed nothing as drastic as that was the case.

I got my dagger ready and unzipped the door of my tent.

Then I waited and listened. Listened for voices or conversation or footsteps or anything that would give me a hint about what had happened out there. My own breathing, as light as I tried to keep it, was deafening.

Moving slowly, I pushed the door of my tent aside, but I didn't lean out. There was a chance, after all, that my toenail cutting had spared me and I didn't want to negate that by stepping outside the protected zone. Instead I dragged the door flap aside and stayed back, surveying what I could see from where I stood.

The bodies of two soldiers lay on the floor of the treasury, and I couldn't tell if they were dead or alive. One lay in a dark splotch of blood left behind by the murder of the Sidhe.

They were both men, and as I craned my neck, I saw the boots of a third soldier. From this angle I could also see part of one of the first two soldiers' hands and part of the other's face. They had multiple dark sores on the skin, each about the size of a quarter. Vainly I stared at their ribcages, willing them to rise and fall, but they were too far away for me to see for sure.

The sores hinted at a plague of some kind. I'd seen plagues before—tons of them. Nothing that had moved this fast, though. The worst I'd seen were akin to Ebola, devastating and contagious, but even that one required physical contact and took hours for the symptoms to develop.

This one behaved like it was airborne and had knocked people down in seconds. Though, perhaps it wasn't airborne. If it was, I'd be dead once I opened my tent. No, this was something supernatural and demonic.

I looked at the time on my phone and saw I'd slept a lot longer than I'd thought. The mages were likely here and would have had time to open the portal. Mouse had probably not wanted to tell me for fear that I'd wake up and refuse to go back to sleep again. That was fair, but I was still angry.

I zipped up my tent and began to pace, four steps each direction, my shoes swishing against the tent floor, my phone clutched in my hand. The newsfeed for Jordan was way too slow to load.

It took me several minutes and a lot of reading to find what I needed. The traditional media was no help quite yet. Social media, on the other hand, had begun promulgating pictures of people struck down with sores on their skin. It appeared the effect was radiating out from Petra into nearby towns in Jordan. It didn't kill absolutely everyone; there were people alive and able to post pictures. It was as if the infection moved through an area and left it behind; survivors who streamed in afterward weren't affected.

I still didn't want to risk stepping outside this tent, though. If this really was originating from the portal, whatever was causing it could still be happening here. Besides, this wasn't the first time I'd been pinned down like this, so while I found it stressful, I could deal. I'd survived every time until now. (I suppose a lot of people think that right before they die...)

A rush of air preceded Aline bursting into my tent. She looked a lot better than she had the last few times I'd seen her. She'd had a shower and her clothes were clean. "How did you do that?" she demanded.

"Do what?" I asked.

"Everyone out there is dead."

"Excuse me?"

"Or... lying down at least."

"I heard screams. I saw the bodies. I hoped they weren't dead." I went to open the door again.

But Aline grabbed my arm. "So, like, I only got a glimpse when I was portalling. I can only see enough to pick where I land, and everyone else was lying down and has, like dark marks on their skin, and you're here, just fine. Oh, and the portal's open."

"Where are the mages?"

Aline frowned. "Dead, I think. They did the spell and then started to collapse and I—I... um. I portalled away. Reflex. I wanted to take them with me, but they had me stand back for the spell and I couldn't reach them and I couldn't push them through the portal..." Tears welled up in her eyes.

"Hey," I said. "You need to survive this. It's good of you to try to save others, but you did the right thing. The portal is definitely open, though?"

"Yeah."

"Okay, so here's what I've figured out, then. This has to be a demon invasion. I put up a ward on this tent."

"Oh, that's how you did it? You set up a demon warding spell? The mages did that too. It didn't work."

"I... probably put up a different one. It was a shot in the dark, what I did."

"Do demons cause pestilences? Like, ones that move really fast?"

"I'm not sure," I said. "Demons suck the life out of people one way or another. My guess is that this invasion, they're sucking the life out of people so fast that they're not sticking around to possess the bodies. With the last tamer of demons in the demon realm, that opens the door to another form of demon coming through. If they've found some way to exist in our world and affect people without stealing human bodies..." There could be millions of them out there and we wouldn't know, and wouldn't be able to defend ourselves.

Aline's wide eyes portrayed fear, but not a full understanding of the implications of what I was saying. Well, that was good. This kid was dealing with enough.

"Can you portal me to the demon realm?" I asked. "Just take me there and get yourself to safety?"

"I can't portal you from right here."

"Then to the nether-world and—"

"Even if I take you to the nether-world, we have to come back here before I can take you into the demon realm. Closest place is five feet over there." She pointed. "There's no way to get there without leaving the tent, and it looks like if we leave the tent, we're dead."

"Can you portal the tent?" I suggested.

"Um..." She considered that. "I can try? Will the protection come with us?"

"Protections go with other temporary dwellings, like what nomads use," I said. I put my hands on her shoulders and looked into her light brown eyes. "You are amazing, and I appreciate everything you've done. Please try to get me into the demon realm, if you think you can do it safely." I didn't want to leave that loophole open, but it was only fair.

The girl stared around the tent. "Yeah, I'll get you to Liana. Let's run at that wall and shove it." She pointed.

We stood at the far wall, got ready, and on Aline's mark we both dashed across the fabric floor and smacked into the wall of the tent.

Which lurched and then dropped about two feet onto a hard surface that stung the soles of my feet and jarred my knees and back. Well, we probably only dropped a few inches, but when you're inside a tent that's falling, it feels much farther.

Aline unzipped the door and peered out. "Nether-realm," she confirmed. "Crazy that that worked!"

I couldn't help but grin. "Okay, once more and to the demon realm. You then get to safety."

"That wall." She pointed.

We got the best lead we could and went full speed at that wall.

Then everything happened so fast I couldn't process it. I felt us falling, and I saw sores appear on Aline's face and felt them appear on my arms. By the time the tent hit the hard ground, she collapsed like she'd been shot, but she reached out and shoved me on the way down. I was knocked spinning again, into darkness, dimly aware that I was on my way to the demon realm, and the tent had not protected Aline.

TWENTY

Think, I ordered myself as I fell through darkness. Be Liana. My girl could remain the rational nerd while the world crashed down around her. The first thought I had was that I couldn't go check on Aline without being struck down myself. The second was that I hated this cold, hard, logical fact. I was okay with them in the heat of battle, but this was different.

Nevertheless, I had to look ahead, not back.

There wasn't a ton that I knew about the demon realm, but I at least knew the general lay of the land on the other side of the portal, and the plagues on Earth suggested to me that there might be a lot of demons pushing on through.

My feet hit the ground and suddenly I was in a crowd of glowing figures, all of whom were pushing past me. I threw my weight forward and turned sideways to weave my way through. The press of bodies had a ghostly quality to them. They weren't warm, and their flesh had no give. They had no scent, not of body odor or soap or anything else. It was as if they were each made of solid air.

A few pairs of black eyes turned to glare at me, but most gazed forward, as if drawn like moths to a flame.

The place was also way too silent, given the large crowd. There was no shuffle of feet against the ground or rustle of clothing as the horde pressed together.

I looked up and saw the stone arch of the portal above me, and beyond that, I saw a dark sky full of unfamiliar stars. The arch was about two feet over my head.

I could jump that. With a leap forward, I shoved everyone back and caused an explosion of shouts in protest, breaking the eerie quiet. Then I did a standing jump straight up, my hands slapping against the cold stone of the portal. I hadn't gotten as high as I wanted—I was barely able to curl the tips of my fingers over the top.

But again, I kept my brain moving even as the situation unspooled. I couldn't pull myself up, so I swung my legs and vaulted up and on top.

Below me, the crowd resumed pushing through the portal, entering one side of the arch and fading until they disappeared on the other side.

I was on a very steep part of the edifice, having emerged far to one side of the portal rather than in the center. That was lucky, because the center of the portal meant the tallest point of the arch, which was a good thirty feet up. I could not have jumped that high.

The stone felt substantial under me—it was cold and solid and real, though my hands made no sound as their flesh slapped against it.

I climbed, clawing my way up towards the top of the arch and hoping that the demons streaming past below wouldn't look up, or care even if they did. The crowd resumed its silence. Those shouts of protest when I'd shoved into everyone had dissipated into the air.

As I climbed, I looked around. The strange sky of stars overhead was what I'd expected. There was the stone platform below, also expected, and there was the appearance of stars far down below the platform. That also matched the descriptions I'd seen about the Starlight Kingdom. I hadn't known how literally to take them; most of what I'd read had been in ancient poetry and verse, so it was hard to say what was metaphor or not.

Below me, the crowd of demons spread to the edge of the platform, with new ones emerging up over the edge constantly. Not a single one of them coughed, shuffled, or wore shoes with soles hard enough to strike the platform audibly. It was distancing, like watching a movie with the sound off.

The surrealness was distancing too.

As I made my way to the top of the arch, I saw I wasn't alone. Someone else was sitting on the keystone with what looked like a file in his hand, and he was sawing away at the rock.

Did him trying to destroy the portal mean he was on my side? The side of Earth and mortals? As I climbed into view, he looked up, and I blinked. He was familiar.

His skin was a lot darker than mine, and his hair long and flowing down his back. His eyes were pitch black, showing he was definitely a demon, and his body was willowy and lanky.

His clothes, though, were blue jeans and a long sleeved shirt. Nothing like the robes all the other demons wore. This guy knew something about Earth, recent Earth.

The expression on his face was one of pure anguish. His hands stilled at the sight of me and he moved into a defensive position. I noted his form was good and he braced himself for a fight exactly like I would have.

"Hi," I said.

"Stay back." His words were startling and demonic and nearly knocked me off my perch.

I heard him speak in English, and Greek, and Arabic, and Gaelic, and Yoruba, and every other language I remembered or slightly remembered, all at once. Unlike the wordless shouts from the crowd below, this was like being punched in the brain with an iron gauntlet.

Pentecost, I thought, remembering the accounts of that day after Christ's ascension. It was a strange tale in the Bible of people appearing to be on fire and speaking a gobbledygook that every listener heard in their own language.

This, I figured, was like that language, a mode of communication that anyone could understand and everyone would find unnerving.

I took a couple of deep breaths to recover. "I'm just trying to avoid getting trampled," I said. "Or arrested or taken prisoner or... any of that kind of thing." My words came out in plain English.

"I never found you funny, Corban."

I chuckled, more out of nervousness than anything else. This wasn't a situation I'd ever foreseen. None of the accounts of the previous expedition mentioned it. "So it's you," I said. "My passenger for two thousand years."

"It's me." He went back to sawing on the portal.

"I'm glad you made it back here."

"Are you? I'm only here for as long as you are. The shackles that bind us haven't been severed."

"But you came back before I arrived."

"Yes... that wasn't pleasant. I came through, the portal closed, and I was nearly torn asunder. Fortunately you stayed near the portal, and now that you're here, it appears I will live."

"You nearly died?"

He turned those black eyes towards me once more, the lids drawn down in a scowl. "Probably not. Such things don't happen here. Pardon me for being dramatic."

That he certainly was. He'd used words approximating "torn asunder."

"The portal wasn't open when you left here the first time," I pointed out. "You would have just been pulled back to Earth."

"I am aware of that," he snapped.

That was enough of the small talk. "Where's Liana?" I asked. "Safe."

"Can I see her? Can you tell me where to find her?"

"Xiii has her."

I waited, hoping he'd elaborate.

"He'll find you soon enough," he said. "He'll probably throw you in the same prison cell."

I gripped the stone arch beneath me, grateful that something in this forsaken place felt real. "Xiii is an individual, then? What does he want with Liana?"

The demon didn't respond or even look up. He kept sawing away with the file, which was also oddly silent. There should have been a pathetic scrape-scrape-scrape sound as he took on the stone edifice with a little metal strip.

As much as I wanted to tear this realm apart to find my beloved, the wisest thing to do was to see if I could get this creature on my side. He was my only solid lead.

"Will cutting down this arch close the portal?" I asked. "And if it will, can I help?"

"I have no idea," said the demon. "I figured it was where I'd start. Knock down the arch, then maybe the ziggurat, then maybe start piling rocks on top."

"You got anything more efficient than a file?"

"I'm too weak to conjure much." He kept on filing.

"Is there anyone else we could ally with who could... ah... conjure—"

"Oh, I didn't think of that," he snapped. Sarcasm sounded very strange in this language he spoke. "The people here don't want the portal closed, obviously." He gestured down at the crowd pushing on through the arch. None of them so much as glanced up at us. "The ones who want the portal closed are all petitioning Xiii."

He paused and looked at something past me, and before I could turn to see what it was, he threw the file at me. "You work on the arch," he said. "And thanks for the help."

I caught the file and nearly lost my balance, but managed to keep my perch with a wild flail of my arms. The metal tool was cold against my skin. Substantial, like the arch itself.

The demon leapt off, sailing away into the darkness, his glowing figure disappearing over the edge of the ziggurat below. I had only fractions of seconds to take all this in, because when I turned, they were on me. This silent world had allowed them to dive at me without even the sound of air rushing under their wings.

TWENTY-ONE

Negotiation really wasn't my strong suit.

I counted at least three demons bearing down, and they could fly. They had great white, feathery wings folded as they dove at the portal. Their first target was the demon who'd just fled, but he was too fast for them, so all three of them adjusted course for me, slamming into me like a wall of air with grasping hands that tried to pin me down.

They were clearly more powerful than I—I couldn't sprout any wings myself. They should also have been, if what we understood about the demon realm to be true, ancient beings with millennia-long lifespans already. They should have been so far advanced in their combat skills that they would pin me on the spot with minimal movements.

And yet, I was able to roll and throw them off easily.

The only problem was that there was nowhere to roll to when perched atop a narrow arch and so I fell.

Faces from the crowd below tilted up to me, little pale ovals directed at me like oblong satellite dishes. They watched me fall, but no one did anything. At least I was falling clear of the fading demons leaving the realm. I wasn't sure what would happen if I fell on or through those.

I relaxed my body, preparing for impact with the harsh stone below. I could survive a fall from thirty feet onto stone; people could do that if they knew how to drop and roll and dispel the force of the fall.

Liana could probably explain it scientifically. I only had a rough idea of how all this worked.

But impact never came. As I neared the platform, I slowed, like the air had thickened below me, or I was on a bungee cord, only I didn't snap back upwards. Instead I landed softly and securely without so much as a jammed toe. No death in this realm, I remembered.

None of the watching demons seemed surprised by this. Those piling through the portal returned their attention to marching on, pouring into oblivion right before my eyes.

The three who'd come after me still stood atop the portal, their wings flared slightly for balance as they glared down at me, hands on their hips. With the wings, they really did look like angels, save for the creepy black eyes.

Nothing I'd read about the demon realm indicated there were angels with white feathery wings over here. Those weren't even in the original, Judeo-Christian tradition; they were interpretations laid atop Biblical descriptions of angels by my Greco-Roman culture.

Such winged angels had not yet been a thing the last time humans came to the demon realm.

Gamlat, I realized. Here was evidence that someone else had come here from Earth in the last few hundred years or so—which fit the timeline of when Gamlat disappeared. It wasn't conclusive proof that she was here, of course, but it was circumstantial evidence that someone else from Earth was.

Or maybe they'd pulled this idea from Liana, assuming these were the same force or faction that had taken her. The arch-sawing demon said that this "Xiii" would catch me before these guys showed up. That meant I didn't necessarily want to escape these henchmen, but I didn't want them to just grab me and haul me off, either.

I stepped away from the arch, keeping my eyes on them. I stuck the file in my back pocket—it could make a weapon of sorts and while it wasn't the same weight or balance as a gladius, I felt confident I could use it as such. My ferrum dagger was still strapped to my forearm.

"Come with us," one of them demanded, a man with very broad shoulders and a square jaw. "We'll take you to your lover."

The three of them all snickered, like fourth graders grappling with the concept of love and finding it ridiculous. It stood in odd contrast to their majestic forms.

They still didn't dive at me. It was as if they'd been tasked with capturing me, but weren't fully into it, like teenagers who didn't fully understand the point of what they'd been told to do.

I was starting to see a pattern.

As much as I needed to see Liana, I needed to figure out a few other things as well. I backed towards the edge of the ziggurat and peered down. The sides were steep, but did have stairs. They were shallow, though, each one no more than four inches deep. It would take a very long time to climb down them. Despite the crush of the crowd pushing for the portal, everyone stayed on one face of the ziggurat. No one came up the sides or back looking to push their way to the front of the line.

The three winged ones saw me looking over the edge and began to move, swooping down towards me.

I jumped over the edge. Since I couldn't die, I had no reason to take the stairs.

But, once I launched myself, I had plenty of time to mull over what I'd done. No death didn't necessarily mean no pain or injury. The slow fall might have been an artifact of being near the portal. My three pursuers weren't in any hurry to go after me, which either meant that they didn't expect me to come to harm, or they didn't care if I did.

The sensation of falling was surreal. I had the feeling of dropping, but there was no wind whipping past my ears or through my hair. It was as if I was in a virtual reality simulator, not a real place.

That lessened my fear, and gave me what I needed: time to think. I'd lived through hundreds of human societies and cultures—I could figure this one out too, if I only gave myself space to do that.

Sure enough, I didn't crash into the stairs as my fall took me near them, but rather slowed again, giving me time to push off and continue my free fall on down. I couldn't tell how tall the ziggurat was—it was hard to eye distances without knowing how clear the visibility was or how big the structures below me were.

So I couldn't say if this ziggurat was a half a mile or a mile high. It was tall, and the ground below changed and shifted as I fell. What had looked like large, blotchy stars now got larger and blotchier and resolved themselves into glowing buildings. Each was in a walled compound with gardens and courtyards. Between each edifice, was pitch darkness.

It wasn't even clear if there was a ground, per se, or an emptiness that I'd fall through for eternity. Previous expeditions reported being able to walk around, so I was banking on there being a ground.

And I was right. I slowed again and was deposited onto blank darkness. When I knelt and pressed my hands to it, it felt like smooth obsidian, but to my eye, it was nothing at all. Pure void.

Looking up, I watched my pursuers glide down. They were being slow and cautious, as if they weren't sure what other tricks I might pull. They were behaving as if they had all the time in the world to catch me, because they did. They were immortal and this place might not be outside of time, but it also wasn't chained to it the way that Earth was. If people here didn't die, there wouldn't be much urgency to get things done. If my capture happened now or a week from now, that was "immediately" to an immortal.

What looked to me like them slowly taking stock of the situation, to them would be lightning fast.

I ran for the nearest compound, which looked like a great, glowing Castle Grayskull sticking up out of the darkness. It was hard to describe it any differently. The compounds I could see farther off weren't of any consistent style or culture or era. In the middle distance was what looked like a Roman villa. Beyond that, Chinese extended family quarters—from about a thousand years ago.

But this wasn't a culture I knew. My best association was the eighties toy and cartoon. And yes, I knew my He-Man cartoons well. I'd watched them all, many, many times. They were entertaining, and had lessons on values and virtues that I found clever, even if they were a little trite.

This Castle Grayskull had no drawbridge or other form of door. While my pursuers meandered after me, I strode right into the castle, like I owned the place, and started looking for the owner.

He wasn't hard to find; he was seated in the courtyard, staring off into space. When I came striding in, he looked up. He had long black hair tied back and a long black beard. His body was stocky and his shoulder muscles bulged. He would definitely fit into the He-Man universe, and I wondered if this meant there was some other deeper truth to that franchise beyond the values it taught.

Corban, I thought, you're losing it, here.

At the sight of me, the man didn't say anything, only stared.

"Hello," I said.

"Hello," he replied in the demonic-all language.

"May I have this castle?" I asked.

He blinked, then shrugged. "I like it. I will keep it." He did nothing to expel me, though.

Yes, okay, I was getting a pretty clear picture of what I was dealing with. When I opened my mouth to say something more, though, the light changed and the demon's face became stricken. The world around us began to brighten and he fled inside, his feet and robes making no noise as he ran.

TWENTY-TWO

The light was shifting, but very slowly. Alone in the courtyard, I took a look around.

There was a stream of glowy water that ran through long grass and over rough rock, very much in keeping with the rough-hewn look of the place. The demon had been sitting on a bench of knotty wood, and off to my left was a little grove of fruit trees.

I wondered if this demon had to eat, and if he did, was it a diet of fruit and water only? Was the fruit on those trees edible for flesh and blood creatures like me?

The place seemed empty, but I reminded myself that most sounds didn't carry here. If there were cooks bustling away in a kitchen somewhere or a baker kneading bread, I wouldn't hear that. Still, this place didn't just sound empty, it felt empty, which begged the question, why was it so big? What were all the buildings, and the rooms in the buildings, for?

Were there any bedrooms? Did demons sleep? Because vampires and angels on Earth did not. If there was no need to sleep and no need to eat and endless time to live, what would they do to fill that time?

The world around me kept brightening and became... more substantial? I hadn't thought of the bouldery structures around me as anything less than solid, but now they looked more solid, more real.

Then I heard it, the soft burble of the water flowing through the courtyard, tumbling over rock and plashing its way through the low arch in the wall that looked like it went to an aquifer. The leaves of the trees also rustled softly.

I also heard the sounds of the owner of this place moving around inside. I could hear his footsteps and the sound of his pushing what sounded like furniture across the floor. Building a barricade, perhaps? Against what?

The walls of this place were rough rock, so it was easy enough to scale one and stand atop it. There was no sign of my pursuers.

I had to scan the horizon until I found what I was looking for—from here the horizon looked like a line of white light, all the dwellings compressed into the skyline.

But as I pivoted, I found a spot where a white bulge jutted up from the horizon. I blinked, then watched as the moon rose.

The tamer of demons shall set them free, and the moon has risen over the starlight kingdom. That was the prophecy that had brought us here. Otuo had fulfilled the first half of it it, or so we thought. The mysterious first tamer might have fit it as well. In any case, for most of my life, the first half of the prophecy was all anyone had ever heard. Then Liana had tamed her demon, and the prophecy had changed. That second line was added on.

That prophecy was uttered by every angel as they ascended, so we all noticed when they began to utter a second line.

I pivoted around some more, looking for my pursuers, and found them huddled atop the portcullis of this castle, curled into balls of fear, wings over their faces. The moon rising was clearly a new phenomenon here; it'd been happening for four years if time here moved parallel to Earth, but perhaps it shocked them anew each time. If things were one way for eternity, and then changed abruptly, even four years would feel like less time than a blink of the eye or a pulse of a heartbeat to a mortal.

Humans on Earth in the middle of an earthquake might relax a little as the ground shook, but still panic anew when the shaking grew worse. Everyone here was experiencing an earthquake like event, the bedrock of their reality shifting abruptly, and they were now being reminded of that all over again.

With a start I realized that if time didn't move parallel, here, Liana could have arrived months or years ago. Crossing with a coyote's help ensured I had stayed on the same timeline—without slippage when I portalled. Liana had crossed on her own, though, and all bets were off.

No, I told myself. Calm down. That demon sawing away atop the arch hadn't made much progress. It couldn't have been that long since he'd arrived.

Unlike the rest of the inhabitants here, he had a sense of urgency, of scarcity of time. His two millennia in mortality might also have been short as a gasp in his immortal reckoning, but it would have been an ongoing calamity far more devastating than a moonrise.

I regarded my pursuers a moment, then climbed along the top of the wall towards them, my scrabbling noises enough to make them peek out from behind their wings.

"Where do you want to take me?" I asked.

"To Xiii," said one.

"Is Xiii a person?"

"Xiii is our leader." He lowered his wings and gave me a contemptuous look. He didn't have the concept of people being from elsewhere stamped into his mind either. My not knowing Xiii was de facto proof that I was an idiot.

"And you'll take me to Liana?"

"Yes."

Given all the information I'd gathered, I strongly suspected these creatures didn't have the habit of lying either. Again, it made no sense in a world with endless time; deception was, by and large, a shortcut to get what one wanted when they didn't have the time to do it the honest way.

The other two had lowered their wings and were glaring at me.

I could run from them. I could hop from house to house, and odds were with all the demons pouring out into Earth, some of them would be unoccupied. These three would only put so much effort into catching me because my being caught by them was an inevitability.

But Earth didn't have time for me to run around exploring, and neither did Liana.

"All right," I said, "you can arrest me." I feared they'd insist on waiting for the moon to set first, but apparently I was enough of a novelty for them to act even while the bedrock of their world kept shifting.

"I take it you can't fly," said one of them.

"Not that I know of."

The three of them all shook their heads and the leader stepped forward. "I will carry you then."

I nodded. "All right."

He grabbed me around the chest from behind, hoisting me in a bear hug as he leapt up off the portcullis and beat his wings powerfully to begin our ascent. I could see his wings in my peripheral vision, but I couldn't feel any air being stirred by them. Nor did I feel air moving past me as we climbed. Again, it was like VR.

I caught a couple of glimpses of the other two demons flying behind us, but it was hard to get a good look in that direction, and the view of what was ahead soon captured my full attention.

Above us one of the stars began to expand in size, until it was as large as the newly risen moon, then larger, then it filled our entire field of view. I looked down and saw the scattered lights of the starlight kingdom. Above was now a vast field of white.

The demon's grip under my arm didn't feel like pure air this time. I could feel the give of his flesh over bone, but it was still insubstantial.

And yet, flying straight at a wall of white still felt dangerous. It looked like we'd smack into it any minute.

Except we didn't. The only hint I had that we'd reached it was the gradual fading of the stars below. They lightened first, then whited out completely, and we were in a place of utter whiteness—like what online retailers created for product photos, a pure white background with the object floating in the middle of it.

I was the object. Well, me and my captors, at least. We hovered in the middle of a Hollywood representation of an incomprehensible world, like Janet's realm on The Good Place.

Yes, I'd watched all the episodes of The Good Place, too. I didn't agree with everyone who was blown away by the philosophy lessons it delivered, but it at least made people aware that there was such a thing as a study of ethics that had resulted in detailed, robust theories down through the centuries.

My captors still flapped their wings, which I guess meant we were still moving? It was hard to say until a dot appeared in the distance that slowly grew larger and larger.

Apparently we were flying horizontal to the ground rather than straight up from it? It was hard to say without said ground as a reference point. Maybe space had pivoted around us?

My head hurt. I suspected Liana had had an easier time on this journey. She had a modern human's brain and a brilliant one at that. She grasped difficult scientific concepts, which kept her mind unmoored enough from what I considered normal reality to be open to all kinds of strangeness.

The dot proved to be rectangular, and as we got closer, it resolved itself into a door. A metal door with a plain metal knob and no discernible lock. I wondered if they'd gotten the idea for how it looked from Earth, or if my brain was supplying how it would look based on what I was used to on Earth.

Yeah, okay, I had a real headache now. This was all too strange for me.

My captor set me down on what proved to be a floor of sorts in front of the door, then gripped the knob and flung the door open.

Beyond it was what looked like the waiting room of a psychiatrist's office, and sitting in one of the plush chairs with her head in her hands was Liana.

They didn't have to prod me to go inside. I went straight for her.

TWENTY-THREE

The door slammed behind me, sounding like it was made of iron and walling me off in a dungeon. I didn't look back, though. I got a rough sense of the rest of the room in my peripheral vision, but didn't pause to look around.

Liana was curled up in fetal position on a plush chair, her shoulders shaking, and she didn't look up when I entered. I didn't know if she couldn't hear me, or if she was too deep in panic to react.

"Hey," I said, kneeling in front of her chair before I tried to touch her. "Liana."

She shifted to show me one watery, tearstained eye, wide with terror.

"You okay?" I asked. "Did they hurt you?"

Her only response was to blink a few times. Her whole body shook.

My girl was one of the strongest people I knew, but everyone has their breaking point. It made sense to me that wandering into the demon realm by accident, being accosted and hauled off by winged beings, and then held indefinitely in a prison would push her past hers. She likely had no way to tell time here. Logic dictated that she was so far beyond where her friends would ever find her, this was where she would then be trapped for eternity.

"Can I touch you?" I asked.

Her only response was a shaky sigh, then more sobs.

So I moved slowly, putting a hand on her arm, which felt fleshy and substantial and real.

"Did they hurt you?" I asked. "Did they beat you or abuse you?"

She shook her head.

So she could hear me, at least.

It reminded me of when a person got sleep deprived—they would cry uncontrollably, literally unable to stop. There was a good chance Liana hadn't slept while she was here.

"Is it okay if I touch you?" I repeated.

She nodded.

"Can I hold you?"

Another nod.

I carefully pried her out of her seat and pulled her down onto the floor beside me, where I could wrap my body around hers.

Her whole ribcage shook with sobs while I put her head against my shoulder and rubbed her back. She felt solid and real and warm. I didn't care that she smelled like sweat and fear and days on end without a bath or shower. After all the unreality, I clung to her as a scrap of the genuine, a relic from the world I belonged to.

"I found you," I said. "You knew I wouldn't stop until I did, right?"

Another nod, her cheek rubbing against my collarbone.

But still the tears came.

Focusing on her crying would only make it harder to stop, though. In my experience, what she needed was a distraction.

"So," I whispered in her ear, "I've figured out a few things about this place."

A slight catch in her sobs meant she was listening.

"You know how vampires and fallen angels aren't immoral, they're amoral? You know how they don't always do the evil thing, they just can't be trusted not to do the evil thing?"

Another nod, and her sobs softened a notch.

"This place is amoral, and there are no consequences here. Life is eternal and unchanging. It's exactly how you'd expect the world of the demons to be. People here have also existed so long, they don't have much to keep them occupied." I told her about my interaction with He-Man.

Her sobs slackened.

I held her closer, willing her to relax and let her anxiety go. I rubbed her back and shoulders while the hiccups that pummeled her body became softer and softer, then stilled.

I wondered if she'd drop off to sleep, then, or if she was still too anxious for that. Or did our bodies even need sleep here?

"W-what's happening on Earth?" she rasped. Her throat was raw from all the crying.

"Maybe you should get some rest before we delve into all that," I said.

Wrong thing to say, and I knew that, but it wasn't as if I was going to hide even the tiniest scrap of truth from her.

"What happened?" she demanded. "Is there a third form of demon going through the portal? A-a third form of possession?"

I couldn't help but laugh, not in mirth, but in disbelief. Even while trapped here, sobbing, that brain of hers continued to work.

"Demons aren't possessing people. They're just going through the portal," I said.

"And not affecting people at all?"

I sighed.

"What, Corban?" She lifted her head, giving me a full view of her tearstained face. Her eyes were bloodshot and had bags under them. Her skin was still smooth and youthful, but it wasn't as ethereal and flawless as it had been before.

Her demon was definitely gone, and this was how she looked as a mortal.

She was also looking at how I looked as a mortal.

Sensing my scrutiny, she pulled away a little. "What's happening on Earth," she repeated.

"They're just draining people somehow. Of their life-force, for lack of a better term. I don't know if they're killing them or just making them very sick. I have no idea. I'm sorry. I wasn't able to find out."

"Tell me everything," she demanded.

This didn't seem like the ideal time, but then again, there was no ideal time for news like this. My back and tailbone were getting sore from sitting on the carpet and holding her. We reshuffled so that she was next to me, leaning against my chest while I leaned back against the chair.

Then, I told her everything. I began with my tent and how I'd kept it safe by cutting my toenails.

This didn't make her even smirk, let alone giggle. She didn't care that her toenail-clipping theory of keeping vampires out of a house was right. Not while people were dying or being hurt in droves.

"From the door, I couldn't really see the people who were affected. They had open sores on their skin is all I can say. I couldn't tell you whether or not they were breathing."

"All the Sidhe?"

My heart sank. My mind had been too addled to remember that she didn't know about the Sidhe or the mages who'd been called in to replace them. "Okay, so this is a longer story than I realized. Get comfortable."

She shifted her weight and I stretched until the vertebrae in my spine popped. Then I told her in slow, halting tones, about how her roommate had been gunned down by Tobias.

I told her about how the coyote-shifters had been nearly wiped out by infighting.

I told her about poor Aline, who'd had to kill Tobias to save the world.

"Oh no..." said Liana. Like many people associated with tragedy, she didn't freeze up at the news that there had been shootings and murders. That was a road she'd already been down before with her own father. While not immune to it, she was a little tougher than most about it.

She shook her head. "Poor kid. She's gotta regret the moment she went up to talk to Gina in the airport."

"She's saved the world, Liana. I think she knew it, too."

Liana's gaze snapped back to my face. "Why are you talking about her in past-tense?"

"Well... I don't know for certain that she's dead, but..."

"Tell me, Corban."

With a deep breath, I told her the rest of the story. She stared into my eyes the entire time, hers wide with disbelief. Tears welled up and ran down her cheeks, but she didn't sob. Staring me straight in the eye prevented that.

"I tried," I told her. "I swear. I never wanted her to come to any harm. I really thought the protection spell would stay on the tent. It does on tipis and Romany caravans and tiny homes. If the worst has happened, I'm not even sure how to find this boyfriend of hers."

"Husband."

"Excuse me?"

"He has an abusive dad. She married him to emancipate him. And I have his phone number and stuff. But let's hope it hasn't come to that yet. Other demon hosts don't die from being possessed."

"Right."

"And she's a tough kid."

"She is that."

"I would still like to destroy everyone and everything that did this to her."

"Hey, I'm game," I said. "First we need to get out of here."

"Well... I'm not sure we do," she said. "We aren't exactly alone in here." She nodded at something behind me.

The hairs on the back of my neck pricked as I turned around, but the corner she'd indicated was empty.

"Keep looking," she said. "Took me hours to spot it when I got here, and... I just haven't been ready to talk to..."

"Talk to who?" I asked.

"I'm not sure what the appropriate title is," she said. "All the ones I can think of are kind of loaded."

"Is it Xiii?"

"No. Definitely not."

TWENTY-FOUR

The room still looked empty. Mauve walls with a heavy weave wallpaper and a plush carpet that absorbed sound had been paired with cushy, opulent chairs that hugged whoever sat in them, separated by the occasional end table. There was nowhere someone could hide in here, even assuming they were a demon who didn't breathe or shift around in telltale ways.

Even in that case, moonrise had affected this place, too. There was a soft scrape every time I shifted on the carpet, and the place had a slight scent, like wallpaper paste and cleaning supplies.

Low coffee tables—too low and small for anyone to hide under—were set out in the middle of the room with innocuous looking magazines reminiscent of the New Yorker. Whenever I looked more closely at any one of them, though, the reality of what they were slid from my consciousness. I suspected that they were like the language that the demons here spoke, some kind of universal concept that would be whatever the person who read it found accessible.

This place was like an upscale waiting room in every respect other than that it had no receptionist window nor exits. There was no sign of the door I'd entered by. The room looked as if it'd been built with us inside it.

I didn't for a moment doubt that Liana was right about us not being alone, though. She wasn't the type to fantasize, and something had distracted her from things like these magazines on the tables.

Or perhaps the kinds of magazines kept on waiting room coffee tables embodied very shallow concepts that only I would find fascinating.

Liana let out a shaky breath. "I know I need to talk to it, but I haven't felt ready. It's just... it's a lot."

There was a flicker of movement in the far corner of the room. I couldn't say what it was that moved, though. Perhaps it was a flicker of color?

Instinct took over and I put Liana squarely behind me while I got into a crouch. That corner looked empty but no longer felt empty. Liana drew in her breath and I could sense her bracing herself.

The flickers of movement began to coalesce—or perhaps reveal themselves was a more apt term. It felt as if whatever I saw had always been there, I just hadn't known how to see it.

Movements and flickers and hints of eyes and wings pulled in on a central point, and I found myself staring at something that I couldn't look at.

Which I realize makes no sense. There was no other way to describe it. I was staring at something that defied definition, even by my own eyes as I tried to focus them.

"Who are you?" I asked.

No response other than a steady gaze in return. Though it made me feel decidedly unsteady, probing my inadequacies and making me feel transparent in a way that I couldn't cover. It was a bit like feeling naked, but nakedness could be undone. This felt like my modesty was being flayed off me in a way that would never regenerate.

My hand on Liana's forearm tightened until she gasped and squirmed.

"Sorry," I whispered, letting go. I hoped I hadn't left a bruise.

"I'm not sure if it's supposed to be here. If Xiii dumped us here with it on purpose or..." She sniffled. Her voice was less shaky now, though. Her resolve had firmed up.

I looked around the rest of the room again. This was supposed to be a place of comfort, clearly.

"I am not an invader," said the presence. "I am always here. People find their ways of overlooking me, but I am always here."

These words sliced through me, burning their truth like acid. The creature spoke the Pentecostal language of the demons, but more intensely. It was as if it spoke more than all the human languages. All the languages humans ever could or would create, perhaps. Or maybe it encompassed languages beyond human. Its speech made my head feel like it would explode.

"Why aren't you letting us overlook you now?" Liana whispered. "Maybe I was good with that arrangement."

A quaking overtook the room, a shivering motion that got into everything, even the spaces between the atoms of my body, and shook them in a way that made me feel like I was going to fly apart. I couldn't help but wrap my arms around myself the way Liana had.

"Are you laughing?" I demanded.

"Humor is a matter of perspective."

"Is her pain funny to you?"

"Corban," said Liana.

"Funny? No... That is not the word."

I shrank back, pushing Liana against the chair.

"Do you want to hurt us?" I asked.

Silence again, and it was a deep silence. An eternal silence. Every second felt like a flicker of endless time.

This presence was over-attentive, focusing on me in a way that drained me. And yet, I knew I shouldn't look away.

"What do you want?" I asked. "You revealed yourself to us for a reason. What is it?"

The creature stirred again, opening itself up like a giant maw, reaching for us.

I turned and pulled Liana into my arms as the room around us shifted. The walls dissolved and the ground became uneven beneath our feet. I got the sense we were standing on grass, but also the sense that it was my idea that I be standing on grass.

We were in a lush place full of plants, and the plants I saw were the ones I chose to see. I was looking at the visual version of the demons' language. I was standing in a concept.

Two figures coalesced nearby, oblivious to our presence. They stood, side-by-side, male and female. The female turned to us. Her eyes were brown, as was her hair. Her skin was medium tone, and she had high cheekbones and broad shoulders.

"Saf," echoed in my mind.

Beside me, Liana stiffened. She'd heard it, too.

And then the vision faded and we were back in the waiting room, the presence drawing back into itself so that it occupied only the corner. Or at least, the part of it we were aware of occupied only the corner.

Although the vision had lasted mere seconds, it still unfolded in my mind like a flower blooming. The richness sending out tendrils that stitched deeper than any naturally formed memory.

"Okay," said Liana, fixing her gaze on the presence in the corner. "Are you willing to show us who you are in all this?"

More of that unnerving, shattering laughter, and then the presence began to shift.

First it threw out beams of light, as if from a multi-faceted prism. Then it began to elongate and to coil.

Right... I thought, as a serpent gathered into form. Its scales were a bronze metallic and its body bent in a figure-eight as it hovered in the air. It's beady eyes stared right at me, and through me, it's tongue flicking out as if to mock me.

And then it was gone and we really were alone. It wasn't the aloneness of an empty room. It was the aloneness of being tossed into a deep well and forgotten for eternity. The only thing that kept me from sobbing was a desire not to look like a fool in front of Liana.

She'd pulled her knees to her chest and was hugging them tight. "Yeah..." she whispered. "Now you know why I didn't feel ready for that." She dabbed at her eyes, her breath ragged and shaky. "What are we supposed to do now?"

I ran my fingers through my hair and then hugged her again. I needed to feel her close—needed to feel the warmth of her body, the quiet thunder of her pulse, the scent of her skin.

She relaxed against me. "Corban, tell me that it isn't our job to give this world's Eve the apple or... whatever. We're not evil, are we? We're from a fallen world but you and I have worked so hard to choose good." She buried her face in my chest.

"We know the tamer of demons concept is wrapped up in the Garden of Eden myth," I said.

Liana nodded. "The first tamer of demons brought evil into the world by building the portal and bringing fallen angels. The second brought vampires. I've released a pestilence on Earth that could wipe out humanity. The answer can't be introducing evil into this world. That's... that's not right. Spreading it around is not right."

"Are you two all right in there?" came a deep, resonant voice from beyond the walls. It also spoke the demon language, but with ease. The words dripped off the tongue like honey. It was as if the other demons were conversant in the language, but this entity was a native speaker. "We've been trying to extract you for quite some time."

Liana sat up. "Why can't you breach the walls?" she called out.

"You have to let me in. I can only help you if you let me in."

"Right, well," said Liana to me, "are we ready for this?"

TWENTY-FIVE

Liana gave me an uneasy look, her arms still wrapped around my waist, her body still pressed against mine. "I'm not sure I can do this."

I kissed her forehead. "Yeah, you can. I believe in you."

With a dubious sigh, she called out, "Come in!"

A door appeared in the wall, a wooden one with a simple, brass knob.

"Can you open the door?" the voice asked.

Liana let go of me and opened the door to admit a man—demon probably wasn't the right word; he didn't even have the black eyes, but rather regular, human eyes that were a deep brown. He was medium height with shoulder length light brown hair and flowing white robes.

"Are you all right?" he asked, rushing in. He didn't touch us, but hovered like an anxious nursemaid.

Liana gave me a wry look.

The man's face fell. "I... am sorry for what happened. I did not expect this place of comfort to be... corrupted in that way."

"Just explain why you locked us up here," she said.

"I didn't," he said. "The angel Jaelyn did, because she thought she would have to in order to curry favor with me. She regrets leaving heaven and going to your world and wants to be let back into my good graces. Obviously, she doesn't need to prove herself for me. I would never be so... transactional."

"Jaelyn is who tried to possess me on Earth?" Liana asked.

"After a manner of speaking, yes."

"So you're Xiii," said Liana.

"I am."

Xiii's robes rustled softly as he stepped farther into the room and looked around. Then with a wave of the hand, he caused the room to dissipate into the whiteness. "Best not to have walls. They are too easy to use for bad ends."

Despite the walls being gone, we could still hear him clearly, as if he was speaking in an enclosed space rather than an endless void.

Two more figures stepped out of the whiteness. One was my friend who'd tried sawing down the portal. He looked chastened, his attention turned inwards. The other was a woman.

Liana looked at them both, her expression betraying nothing.

"Did you manage to cut the portal down?" I asked my former passenger.

"That doesn't work," said Xiii, "but we knocked down the arch again, just in case. No impact on those flooding out of this world to their own damnation." He lifted his shoulder in a shrug.

"No, it will take something much more comprehensive to get that portal shut, but then we can save both of our worlds."

The female demon had fixed Liana with an amused look. "You don't recognize me now, do you? Or Ro?" She pointed to my passenger.

Liana shook her head.

"My demon and yours," I said to her.

"Wait what?" Liana said. "Those demons looked like you and me when I arrived here. It was really, really creepy. You two..." She looked them over; Jaelyn looked nothing like Liana. Her hair was jet black and her complexion dark. Her body was willowy and thin.

Liana now had curves, which I most definitely approved of, though I averted my eyes to avoid approving too much. This wasn't the time.

"It took us a while to remember ourselves," said Ro.

"But you guys decided to keep wearing jeans," Liana observed. "And T-shirts." In fact Jaelyn's outfit was a close facsimile to Liana's own.

"These are comfortable," said Jaelyn. "We'll be keeping them."

"Please," said Xiii, "these are angels, not demons. I know they may seem strange and alien and frightening when they enter your world, but they are innocent souls. It's in both our worlds' interests to close the portal, so let's work together."

"It can be closed?" Liana asked.

"It can. We need only to remove its purpose. Once there is no reason for a portal between our worlds to exist, it will close."

"What's its purpose?" I cut in. As much as I trusted Liana, my curiosity got the better of me. She took a step back, attention focused inward, that brain of hers working away.

"To bring evil into this world," said Xiii.

He waved a hand and the whiteness around us began to dim, until we could see the Starlight Kingdom scattered below, with its softly glowing ziggurat and the hordes of beings—looking like thousands upon thousands of pinpoints of light—still crowding their way to the top, where they disappeared into thin air. The portal was, indeed, still open.

"That is the main evil," he said. "The stealing of our precious souls. And when they come back, those few who do, they are tainted by your world."

"So what do you propose?" Liana asked, her gaze fixed on the scene below.

"This is a pristine world. Yours is a fallen one. As you can see, this world is incomplete. It hasn't been fully created yet. When your world was created, evil entered it and it fell. I want to prevent that from happening to this world."

I looked at Jaelyn and Ro. They stood with their heads bowed. "Are you two Adam and Eve?" I asked.

"Definitely not," said Ro.

"Those are your names for the first fully created, flesh-and-blood humans?" asked Xiii. "No, and these two want to be bound to me, to serve my will. They have sworn an oath to never introduce the evils they've seen into this world and I shall ensure they don't. The first man is a good man who has never encountered evil, and, no offense, must never encounter you."

Liana nodded. "I understand." She looked up at the stars overhead.

"As for the first woman... the one who is supposed to take that role, according to prophecy, is one of the most corrupt creatures in this world."

"Saf?" Liana asked.

"Yes, that is her name. She spent a very long time in your world and it changed her. You humans describe her as evil, and therefore I trust that's what she is. She should not be the first woman."

"If she spent a long time in our world," Liana said, "did she possess a human woman named Gamlat?"

"Yes," said Xiii.

"Gamlat returned to this realm, then?" I asked.

Xiii turned to me and nodded. "Yes, and in order to close the portal, we must neutralize all evil within our realm. Once it isn't possible for evil to enter this world, the portal will close and we remain pristine. Unsullied. Heaven."

"How do you neutralize all evil?" Liana looked at Ro and Jaelyn dubiously.

"Yes well, I suppose that part may be difficult to sell," said Xiii.

Both Jaelyn and Ro looked down at their feet.

Xiii frowned. "We find Saf and send her back through the portal."

"And that closes it?" asked Liana.

"No. If it did, the portal would have closed the last time Saf was gone and we'd banished everyone else from your world. She needs to go to your world so that she can die there. There is no death here. Once she is dead and these two bound to me, the portal will close."

Liana nodded. "So you want me to kill the third and final Nabatean vampire."

"Yes," said Xiii. "You're no doubt up to the task."

I shook my head. "Before Gamlat came back here the first time, she was an angel. Before she came back the second time, she was a vampire. What if, when she goes through the portal, she becomes the third kind of demon? An agent of this pestilence sweeping Earth with no human host to kill?"

"I will provide you with the necessary spell to bring all such entities into corporeal form."

"So we can kill them all?" asked Liana. "Since you can't let anyone who's been over in Earth come back?"

Xiii shut his eyes, and it took me a moment to catch on to the fact that he was fighting back strong emotion. When he opened his eyes again, a glistening tear slid down his cheek. "That is why I want this portal gone as soon as possible. If I could give them a chance to bind themselves to me, I would, but it won't be possible."

"Why not?" Liana asked.

"Because to bind these two to me, I need something from you and you will be banished as soon as we expel Saf. I need your blood. As I'm sure you're aware, the blood of a fully created human has power."

"We are willingly volunteering to be bound to him," said Jaelyn. "It's the only way to ensure we never bring evil to this world."

"Our faith is in him," added Ro.

They both fixed Liana with earnest glances, and when she looked uncertain, they also looked at me.

"Okay... I've heard enough to know what to do, here." Liana turned to me, one eyebrow raised, her silent way of asking if I needed any more information.

I had a million questions I wanted to ask, but I nodded nevertheless.

Liana faced Xiii and said, "Get thee behind me. You lie and I will never help you in your scheme to find Saf and bring about the fall of this world."

"But..." said Jaelyn.

"This," said Liana, gesturing at Xiii, "is not your Savior. This is the destroyer."

TWENTY-SIX

Xiii shook his head. "I suppose I can understand your being confused. Do you not know who tried to corrupt you in the waiting room?"

"Yeah..." I said. "She knows."

"I know who it was an agent of. And I know what a real angel looks like," said Liana.

The floor beneath us began to rumble and shift as Xiii's form began to morph. He sprouted white wings and his skin began to glow gold.

Liana shielded her eyes and stumbled over to me, wrapping an arm around my waist. "Right?" she whispered.

"Yeah, you got it right," I said.

"Why's he still so pretty?"

"He can dress up how he wants," I said. "Doesn't change who and what he is."

"That-that serpent," Xiii spat. "How could you follow him?"

"The brazen serpent?" Liana asked. "I decided to look and live."

She was referring to a story in Exodus, when poisonous snakes had overrun the Israelites' camp and people were dying from their bites. Moses had raised up a bronze serpent and told his people that if they would but look at it, they would live.

Not everyone did, but those who obeyed did, indeed, live.

When the presence in the waiting room had showed us this image, it had been a test. Would we see a serpent and assume he represented evil, or would we know the full story?

"He wants to bring evil to this world," Xiii argued. "He's allowed evil to have constant access to this world."

"So you say," said Liana. "You're not who we trust." She let go of me and stood up straight and proud, no mean feat as the floor continued to shake.

"You are children of hell!" Xiii shouted.

"No," I said. "We're just doing our study abroad there."

With a deafening crack the floor tilted to one side, steep enough that I lost my footing and fell, smacking my hip hard. I made a wild grab for Liana and she rolled towards me so that we were able to cling to each other as we slid away.

Xiii and his minions had all sprouted wings and now hovered, disappearing into the distance as Liana and I picked up speed. Again, our passage was otherworldly. No air rushing past, not much ambient sound. Just the sickening feeling of falling. I wasn't sure whether Xiii was banishing us, or if we were being rescued from him.

Liana and I clung to each other, doing our best to breathe and not panic. Her fists were tight knots, clutching at my shirt.

"We won't die," I said. "Remember that. We won't even hit the ground hard. I jumped off the ziggurat and was fine."

But she was beginning to hyperventilate, and I couldn't blame her. My words were just words. No matter how much she might trust me, I was telling her that plummeting wouldn't kill her and millions of years of instincts told her otherwise.

The falling feeling, without the wind blowing past, would only be more disturbing to her, not less. Real falling would have caused Liana's hair to whip around and the passing air would have clawed at our clothing. This, after a few moments, felt like a stomach bug, the kind of bug where your stomach was trying to climb your esophagus and pound on the inside of your ribs to say that something was very, very wrong.

Below us, the ground began to dissipate. Rather than being glowing domains and glowing people, the lights began to spread out. It wasn't as if we were rising, though, or it was falling away. The lights were spreading out to look more like the stars above us, and to the sides of us.

Tears overflowed in Liana's eyes.

That was the only thing that grounded me in all this. I wasn't stronger than she was. I certainly wasn't smarter. Nevertheless, if she needed to fall apart right now, I could summon the machismo to comfort her through the process, to pretend like I was in enough control to ensure things would be all right. It was a lie, but that kind of machismo was always a lie.

"Hey," I whispered, inhaling the scent of her neck.

A hiccuping sob.

I kissed her forehead, then her temple, then her cheek—tasting the salt of her tears.

With a gasp she turned her head and pressed her lips to mine, her fingers of one hand curling around the back of my neck. Her other arm gripped me tight around my waist.

I leaned in, pressing her to me and kissing her back, feeling the soft warmth of her lips and tasting more of her salty tears.

Then with another gasp, she pulled back, eyes wide. "I'm sorry."

It took me a second to catch my breath. We hung in the void, now, with dots of light against darkness as far as the eye could see.

I took a moment to take all this in before looking down at her again. "Sorry for what?"

"You know what."

"Um, with everything else going on, I wouldn't worry about going too far with a kiss," I told her. American puritanical thinking often bothered me, especially at times like this. Girls were taught that any situation could escalate, even if she and the guy were drifting through space just after being expelled by Satan.

Give me a break.

Her attention had diverted elsewhere, though. "The stars are disappearing."

I craned my neck and found that this wasn't true in general, but in one, specific direction, there was a great, blobby darkness devoid of stars. And it was growing bigger.

"That... does not seem good," I said.

"We're sure I got it right?" Liana whispered.

"Pretty sure," I said. "Be calm, okay?"

Whether I spoke for her benefit or mine, I couldn't say. With the darkness growing to one side of us, I couldn't tell whether we were falling down or drifting sideways or both or neither. If my stomach hadn't been empty, I suspect I would have vomited.

As it was, I wasn't certain that I wouldn't.

Liana had twisted her body to face the darkness, though. "It's coming towards us."

"That seems bad. I mean... I can see why that would seem bad."

"Do we believe in anything worse than who we just faced?" she chided me.

Only moments ago I'd been confident that I could stay strong while she dealt with the extremity of our situation. How quickly I'd lost track of that goal. I couldn't excuse myself based on a lack of experience as a boyfriend, either. Looking out for mortals like Liana was in my wheelhouse as a guardian angel.

"Sorry," it was my turn to say. "I don't mean to despair."

"Oh, don't say that," she said. "Convince me that you're not despairing."

"It's not in my nature to lie."

"Corban." She dug her fingers into my shirt, gripping it much like she had for that most passionate kiss before I'd killed Melanie.

Focus, the little voice in my head ordered me.

"I'm gonna pray," said Liana, burying her face in my chest.

That seemed like a smart idea. I lowered my head and tried to do the same, but my mind was too addled for me to focus and I couldn't shut my eyes while the darkness loomed closer.

Liana always prayed silently—I'd never heard her utter a single prayer aloud. She was the sort to fold her hands, close her eyes, bow her head, and think her supplication.

Like a great cloud of locusts, the darkness rushed upon us, enveloping us. When Liana opened her eyes, the stars were gone and the world was pitch black.

The only way I even knew she'd opened her eyes was her hesitant utterance of, "Um... this doesn't seem good."

"The darkest hour is just before dawn?" I offered.

"That is the dumbest saying. How did that ever even get to be a saying? You know how many sunrises I've seen? You know the thing about sunrise? It is hard to know the moment it happens unless you have vampirism or are looking in the right direction because it is so light before dawn that—"

"Okay, okay, breathe." I whispered this right against her temple. "I didn't mean to trigger you there. It works as a saying about life. About dark times being worst before things get better."

"Because otherwise the moments after wouldn't count as better, would they?"

Now I'd set her off in another way. I'd stated something plainly logical as if it were profound.

"Truce," I begged. "Please."

"Your phone wouldn't happen to still have battery, would it?"

"Yeah," I said. "Let there be light!"

I got out my phone and tapped the screen, hearing its soft chime.

Liana cleared her throat. "Tempting fate?"

The screen didn't light up. I could feel it under my fingers but the darkness around me didn't lessen at all.

TWENTY-SEVEN

Liana gripped my phone as well, her fingers probing the screen.

I could feel the screen's smooth liquid crystal under the pads of my fingers. Soft beeps and feedback told me that I was manipulating icons and launching apps, but there was no light.

"You got your phone?" I asked.

"The battery died. I tried to preserve it, but I kept wanting to check the time..."

"The backlight on mine must be burned out," I said.

"Or," said Liana, "this is the same darkness that descended during the plagues of Egypt."

"Yeah, I like my theory better," I said.

"Think about it—"

"I don't want to think about it." But of course, I only said that because I had that luxury. I knew that Liana would think about it even if I refused. If there was one thing I could count on Liana to do, it was to think.

"This darkness," she said, "obscured the stars. All those stars probably didn't burn out. There doesn't seem to be any kind of structure around us. During the plagues of Egypt there was a darkness that was so profound that people's lamps didn't dispel it."

"We going to have frogs start plopping down on us?" I asked.

"That came before the darkness and—"

"Okay, stop," I said.

"Sorry." She paused. Then, "I think we've stopped falling, though."

It was possible, though my stomach was far too unsettled to give me a straight answer on that one.

I tapped the lower lefthand corner of my phone screen and then stabbed blindly at the middle. That should have launched my phone dialer, which ought to have brought up my latest calls, which meant I could dial any of those numbers by tapping them.

But when I put my phone to my ear, there was only silence. Then again, there was no reason why I'd have reception here. I switched off my phone and put it back in my pocket.

Liana had shifted her grip to the front of my shirt, and with one hand she reached out into the darkness, only to snatch it back suddenly.

"Did you feel something?" I asked, the hairs pricking on the back of my neck.

"No, I felt nothing, and that creeped me out. Feeling something... would be even worse." Her voice was thin with fear.

Her being scared made me scared. If she was struggling, then how could I figure out what to do? There was no obvious way to fight our way out of this.

Stop it, I ordered myself. No spiraling.

Liana's arms were wrapping around me again. "So... um... kissing to distract me right now, would that be okay with you?" she whispered.

I nodded, wondering if she could tell which way my head was moving. A better, answer, I decided was to lean down and kiss her.

Her return kiss was timid, hesitant, as if she was afraid of appearing too enthusiastic about it.

While a part of me certainly wanted to kiss and make out and take the lead, I reined that in.

Instead I took a deep breath and kept the kiss gentle, drawing it out long and loving, focusing entirely on her and how upset she was. It was a good way to distract from how upset I was.

I held her close. She needed to feel like this kiss could go on forever.

Slowly, it worked. The muscles in her back began to slacken and her body to relax. Her arms tightened around me and she broke off the kiss to touch her nose to mine and whisper, "Yeah, okay, I needed that."

"Me too."

A few kisses later, she pulled away, taking a deep breath. "Okay, what are we going to do now?"

"I was hoping you'd have a genius idea."

"And I was hoping you'd have some ancient wisdom."

We managed to say this to each other with humor and not accusation. It was one of those moments that affirmed to me again that I could spend eternity with this woman. Or even better, the rest of my mortal life, if we got out of this with our mortal lives intact.

I felt Liana shrug. "I was just gonna try this." She turned her upper torso away from me and shouted, "Hello!!!"

Yeah, that did make logical sense.

We both listened to the following silence.

Then we heard it. "Hello?" The voice was raspy, hoarse. I was pretty sure it was a woman's voice, and that it came from my left.

"Who's there?" Liana called out.

"Ah... who am I?" The person spoke English, plain English with a slight British accent. None of the demonic Ur-language that tickled the brain. "I'm... ah... I suppose you would know me as Gamlat."

Liana's body went tense against mine.

The name hit me like a punch in the sternum. Even though we knew she was here, meeting her was a shock. The first vampire, Otuo's wife, and the adopted sister of Melanie and Darissa, two ancient, deadly vampires we'd killed, was here in the dark with us.

Great. Just great.

"So you're the human, Gamlat?" Liana asked. "Not the demon who rode Gamlat?"

Silence was the first reply, which gave me time to admit to myself that this was a fair point. The human, Gamlat, had been a benevolent guardian angel for millennia. It wasn't fair to blame her for the acts of the demon that had possessed her.

Since she wasn't replying in English, I tried ancient Arabic—the dialect that had been spoken when I was mortal. I didn't remember it terribly well, but well enough to say, "Gamlat the human?" and hope the question made sense.

The response was a blood curdling scream that made Liana cling to me, her fingers digging into my arms like claws.

"Demon!" the voice shrieked. Then she switched back to English. "I knew you would infiltrate this place. Nowhere is safe! Nowhere!"

Well, that was hypocritical.

"What did she call you?" Liana whispered.

"Demon," I said. Then louder, "I'm human. Before that I was a guardian angel like you were. Like Otuo."

"Otuo..." Her voice flushed with anguish. Then she said another name, and another. None of them were familiar to me, but Otuo had been so old that he'd probably had thousands of names.

"Can you help us?" I begged. "Help us to save Earth from the demon realm?"

"Let me guess," she said, her tone dry. "You turned down Xiii's offer to shut the portal?"

"What offer?" asked Liana. "He was lying."

"He was not lying."

"Wait," I countered. "Don't you know who he is?"

But Liana was clutching me. "Are we sure?" she said in a low voice that Gamlat could probably hear anyhow. "I mean—"

"Yes," I said.

"But think about it," she said. "Maybe I focused too much on shallow stuff, like the color of the serpent and the fact that Xiii is thirteen in Roman numerals."

"Oh," I said. "It is? It's spelled X-i-i-i?"

"Yeah."

"How did you figure that out?"

"I asked," she said. "When I was being kidnapped by his minions I pumped them for information."

Of course she had. That was my girl. Relentlessly practical, even when in a foreign realm and at the mercy of powerful beings. I could imagine her giving her captors the third degree as they dragged her off.

"But the entity there in the waiting room," I said, "wants to finish the creation of this world. It looked like an angel, a real one. A Biblical one."

"And what happens," said a voice right at my elbow, "after the creation?"

Both Liana and I startled. I gripped her tighter against me and felt us start to spin.

"There is a floor," said Gamlat. "If you'd stand, it will support you."

I reached down with my toes, and sure enough, I felt a solid plane to stand on. Never had the term "grounding" made more sense to me. I wasn't floating free in a void anymore. My feet were pressed firmly to a surface that gave me a definitive sense of up and down. The darkness was still oppressive.

Liana's weight shifted and she was standing too.

"We can't conjure, as the natives of this realm do," said the voice. "But simple things I've asked for have been granted. A place to disappear, a floor to stand on, comfort from eons of despair. That one comes and goes."

"How long has it been since you've spoken to anyone?" Liana asked.

"To anyone real? How should I know? I have plenty of visitors, but I suspect they aren't real. When you know that talking to yourself is madness, madness invents other people to talk to. I've spoken to the last tamer of demons countless times."

"You must have your speech to them memorized pretty well, then," I said. "So let's hear it."

"Are you the last tamer?"

"No, I am," said Liana. "Supposedly. I mean... I don't know."

"Yes, that sounds about right," the voice replied. "What I have to say is simple. You have to help Xiii. Everything you thought you knew about right and wrong was delusion."

TWENTY-EIGHT

"Gamlat's insane," I whispered into Liana's ear. "She's been stuck here for over a century."

Liana's muscles were as tense as iron cords under my arm. I massaged her shoulder with one hand and kissed her cheek.

"Why do you think this realm exists?" Gamlat asked, her voice coming from the right this time.

A sigh was Liana's only answer. Not a sigh of boredom or defeat, but one of fortitude. She was bracing herself for what was to follow. "Why are we here in this darkness?" she asked, ignoring Gamlat's question. "How did you end up here?"

"Do you really think you're a savior?" The voice was behind us now. "Do you really think you have the power to deliver a world? That of all the people on Earth, you'd be the chosen one?"

Now my muscles were tensing up. I realized I was squeezing Liana's shoulder and made myself stop.

Gamlat had hit on one of Liana's weaknesses, though. Liana did not think she was anyone special. She often wondered why she was the first half-turned vampire, why nobody else in the past twenty-five hundred years had done what she had.

My pointing out that she'd proven how exceptional she was when she became a half-turned vampire didn't persuade her. It was in her nature to be humble. Normally that was a good thing.

"Why are you here?" Liana repeated.

Yes, I thought. Stay with your line of questioning. Don't let Gamlat steer you off course.

"Otuo was the same," Gamlat's voice said, now distant and echoing. "He didn't think he was anyone special either. Just a man trying to do the right thing. Then again, perhaps those truly are rare on Earth."

Her cackle made me shudder as if spiders were walking up and down my spine.

"So," said Gamlat, now near us and whispering, "why do you think this realm exists? Why do all the different realms connect to Earth as the hub? There are many theories, but I favor the one that says that alternate realms are created by human ideas. They are how humanity works out the contradictions of its existence."

"This realm is pulling the universe apart," I snapped. "It's not just an idea." Then I realized, I'd fallen into her trap. I'd argued with her, engaged with her.

"Ideas can't destroy worlds?" Now she sounded like she stood right in front of us and was smiling with amusement. "Show me a human that doesn't live in a world of ideas, surrounded by objects that began as ideas? Show me a war or catastrophe that doesn't involve human ideas? Whether it's not tolerating people who are different or building cities in places that aren't suited for it, all catastrophes begin and end with human ideas."

Liana put a hand on my chest. Without being able to see, I didn't know if she was reassuring me, or trying to hold me back.

"And you don't see how destructive an idea religion can be?" Gamlat went on.

Now we were on a well-worn track in human discourse. I kept my mouth shut and waited for her to go on.

Only, she didn't. The next beat, when I expected her voice to come from some new direction, passed, as did the beat after. My subconscious had tried to map out where she would be standing next, so the silence left me feeling like I was reaching after something off a ledge and now teetered, precariously balanced, liable to plunge downward at any moment.

Liana began to tremble.

"Hey," I whispered. "Don't let her lame parlor trick of moving around scare you, okay? There's nothing to it. She's just climbing around. If you think about how that looks, it's not scary at all." It was comical, really.

I wasn't sure if Liana had the same amusing image of an old woman climbing around on scaffolding, but her shakes eased up. She gulped down a breath and I rubbed her back.

"So..." Liana said, her voice thin, "you're saying the Judeo-Christian idea of the creation is destroying Earth?"

"Not the creation," said the voice, now below our feet. "A nonsensical view of right and wrong. A blind obedience to one side, even when the other presents a reasonable plan."

"Xiii won't banish Saf," Liana argued. "He lies, and she's his way to corrupt humanity, his back door into creation."

"Indeed?" Gamlat now sounded like she was about ten feet away, shouting. "You forget who Lucifer was before he fell. He was an angel. His name means 'light bringer.' That's who he is here, in this realm. Lucifer, before his fall. He will banish Saf. He wants to banish evil from this realm."

What she said was technically true. Lucifer did mean 'light bringer' and he had started out as an angel. Down through the ages I'd heard many accounts of his fall from grace. None of them dwelt long on who he was before he fell, though; his fall and his role as the avatar of evil eclipsed his previous life.

"It is your God who will not banish Saf," said Gamlat.

Now it sounded like she was lying on the ground behind us, and it was all I could do not to roll my eyes at the image. Though I suppose in the pitch dark, it wouldn't matter if I did. She couldn't see us.

"What does that say about your God?" she pressed.

"Why does He allow bad things to happen to good people?" I asked. "That's the argument you want to have?"

"What you already know," Gamlat whispered into my ear, "is that God was aware the fall could happen. That calamity could strike the moment after creation was finished. Why allow for this? Why give evil a back door?"

"Satan opened that door," Liana insisted. "He's the one who beguiled Eve."

"And the creator of the door is blameless?" Now she was directly over our heads.

"Stop climbing around," I ordered her. "It's not having the effect you want."

"So you're saying," said Liana, "that a God who allows evil things to happen to good people is a paradox that can tear our universe to shreds?"

"Ah, smart girl," Gamlat replied. "Consider how destructive the paradox has been just on Earth. People punishing each other for supposed affronts against their loving God of peace. The belief that suffering is okay because God is just, even though the world most definitely is not. Living in a world that people believe was a mistake, and that is supposed to be ruled by an infallible king. It never made any sense."

"So you think," said Liana, "that we should side with Xiii, expel and kill Saf, and then let this world finish its creation under Xiii's direction?"

"Yes."

I was surprised at the bluntness of the answer. With all the shifting around she'd been doing, I'd expected her to dance around the topic as well.

"And if you believe that your God and Satan are real—" now Gamlat sounded like she was seated in front of us "—then what if Satan has been doing everything he's been doing on Earth to prove to you that evil should have no place in the world? That it always creates suffering and pain?"

Now I did roll my eyes. "What if he's been putting our hands in the fire to show us fire is hot?"

"Yes." For once, she hadn't moved. She was still in front of us.

"Or maybe he just likes torturing people," I said. "Ever consider that?"

"Given all the time I have lived," she replied. "I have been able to devote centuries to considering that, yes. It seems rather pointless, though, for a good God to put us at the mercy of someone who merely likes to torture us."

"So you're saying God isn't necessarily good," said Liana.

"No," I argued. "This realm, under Xiii's rule, isn't heaven. It's a place where nothing happens and the inhabitants are bored out of their minds. They're bleeding out over the edges."

"Corban," Liana whispered. "We really going to argue that evil is the answer to people being bored?"

Fair point.

But Gamlat had a different one. "If your world was stuck mid-creation, you'd get bored too. If you were left in limbo while your creator tried to set up a system where you might fail and evil could corrupt your future, would you not want to escape?"

"No..." I said. "I'm just saying that Xiii doesn't have a demonstrably good plan."

"You may not like this place, but it's a million times better than Earth."

I wasn't making any headway here. I kept my mouth shut and hoped Liana would figure out an answer.

"Hello?" said another voice in the distance.

Liana twisted away from me. "Gina?"

"Liana? Amy's here too." The voice came closer. "Is this the demon realm? Why's it so dark? Where are the stars?"

"Do you guys have a way out of here?" I asked, my heart brimming with hope.

"Um, no." That was Amy. "Pretty sure this was a one way deal for us."

"Ah, so now you're trapped here, too." Gamlat laughed uproariously.

Interlude:

Gina

TWENTY-NINE

*A*fter the battle at the gates of Petra, when we watched the armies of heaven and hell sling energy pulses and lightning at each other...

After our side won and there was a mad scramble of people getting the tanks rolling again...

After Amy and I talked to Corban, then fell asleep in the SUV, waiting on the endless line of soldiers to march into Petra...

After we awoke and found everyone lying like slumped corpses, bruises and sores splitting their skin like they'd been hit with a chain whip...

After we braved leaving the SUV and determined that whatever had gotten everyone else hadn't gotten us...

After we followed the trail of bodies into the park, to the fabled treasury and found the bodies of Siobhan and Mouse...

After all of these things... we found Aline, lying under a crumpled heap of a tent inside the treasury. Her body was covered with bruises and sores, and I was on the verge of screaming. The battle and whatever this plague was were big events, too big for me to get my head around. Her death was smaller, more personal, more devastating. This kid had sacrificed everything for us, and now she was gone.

Amy cried, her head bobbing with sorrow as she knelt by Aline's body. She pressed her fingers to the girl's throat, then gasped. "She's got a pulse."

"You're sure?" I knelt down on the soft folds of the tent, which cushioned against the hard stone floor.

"Yeah, I'm sure. I know how to take a pulse, all right?"

I loved Amy, but she got mean in a crisis. Mean to me, at least. Any minute now she'd start her rant about me being bossy.

"We need to get her to a hospital," I said. "Do we go get a car or do we carry her—"

"Carrying her could injure her," Amy snapped.

"She's sick, not injured."

"Stop trying to take charge!"

I missed Liana right then. She had a vulnerability about her that made it hard to bicker in front of her. Amy and I had been on the verge of breaking the pinkie promise we'd made in kindergarten to always be friends when Liana showed up in our high school. Her arrival had saved it.

Without her, a situation like this was more than either of us could take.

"Just... okay," I said, leaning down to pick Aline up.

Amy put out a hand to stop me.

Aline's body slid to one side, and the floor tilted and the world blacked out. A few blinks later and I came to on the flat plain of the nether-realm. The hospital was off in the distance and Amy was sprawled out behind me, struggling to get to her feet.

Aline lay between us, moaning softly.

"Hey," I said. "You okay? It's me, Gina. Amy's here too."

The girl peeled a bloodshot eye open and regarded me, then whispered, "Carry me towards the hospital."

"What did she say?" Amy asked.

"She wants us to carry her towards the hospital."

My lifelong friend and I exchanged a nervous look.

"Do you think you can treat her there?" I asked.

Amy's mother was a trauma nurse, and Amy had worked summers in the hospital and knew how to do simple things like draw blood and insert an IV.

"Um, I can try," she said. "Can you carry her?"

I was the one who'd been working in a forge for the past several months. My arms had some muscle, and Aline was light, disturbingly light. I gathered her against my chest and lifted her off the ground, her head lolling against my chest. She took a deep breath, which let me breathe easier. For now, at least.

Amy struck out towards the hospital and I followed, carrying Aline. The plain was flat as a board and the sky overhead felt flat as well. The light splotch that served for a sun wasn't visible. The sky to my right was lighter than the sky to my left. We were beyond the world's end.

"D—" Amy began.

But the world went dark again and the ground went soft. I tripped and did my best to keep my balance. I did not want to drop or fall on Aline. This required several running steps forward, from the soft ground onto uneven concrete.

Light blazed around me and I heard the babble of voices before I saw a group of figures rush at me.

"Aline!" cried a reedy, child's voice.

"Is she all right?" a woman with a German accent demanded.

Before I could get my bearings, gentle hands took Aline from my arms

"Wait," I said. "What she has, it might be contagious."

"Diseases don't portal," said a blond woman, the one with a German accent. She and a couple of other women hurried off with Aline.

I looked around and saw I was in a courtyard of a dilapidated apartment complex. Dead, skeletal vines clung to the once white stucco, and the concrete pad under my feet had been cracked, split, and shifted by tree roots. A lone, large tree in the center threw a dappled shade over everything and I heard the rusty squeak of a metal door-guard opening and closing. The group with Aline had gone inside.

Lingering in their wake were three little kids, all under the age of ten, with the unusual coloring that marked them as coyote-shifters. When they saw me looking at them, they darted in the door as well.

I turned around then walked a circle, looking for Amy, and found her disoriented, leaning against the far side of the tree. At the sight of me, she relaxed. "Hey."

"Hi, I think Aline brought us to her kind's secret hideout."

"Diseases don't portal?" she asked. "Does that mean you can cure disease by portalling a person?"

"Please don't ask further questions," said the woman with the German accent. She'd emerged and was walking towards us again. "Sorry to be so abrupt with you, but we need to know what happened to Aline."

WE TOLD THEM everything we knew, which wasn't much. Katarina (the woman with the German accent) theorized that what had happened was demonic, and that Amy and I were spared because we had ferrum in our blood. It seemed as good a theory as any.

Once she finished interrogating us, Katarina made sure we were fed and got showers, then offered us beds in an empty apartment. I had no idea what time it was, but was exhausted enough to fall straight to sleep.

When I woke up, it was dark and Amy was awake, sitting up on her bed, watching me.

I stretched and sat up as well. The beds were minimal but comfortable, with clean smelling sheets and thin blankets. The climate here was more like New York than New Mexico (I hadn't been many other places).

"I want to look around," said Amy. "But I'm not sure if I dare."

"And you want me to be your cover?" I asked. "If we get caught, you want to blame me?"

"Si."

"Bueno. Vamonos." I rolled out of bed. We'd worn the terrycloth bathrobes we'd been provided after our showers to sleep and had washed our underwear in the bathroom sink with shampoo. My undies were still a little damp, but I pulled them on along with my still filthy clothes. Amy did the same.

The apartment complex was a lot cleaner on the inside than the outside. The carpets looked new, and not far from our room was a shared kitchen with state of the art appliances. Lights came on with a motion detector system, so there was no sneaking around. People would know someone was traipsing the halls.

I had the distinct impression we were still in the United States, but what did I know?

Most of the doors along the hallway were closed, and because we knew people lived here, we didn't go testing the knobs. The entire place was four hallways that enclosed the central courtyard, and was two stories tall. Besides the kitchen, we also found a media room and a small gymnasium with a gleaming wooden floor. One of the apartments that wasn't shut up tight appeared to have been converted into a classroom.

We couldn't find Aline, but she was probably behind one of the closed doors.

Amy nudged doors as we walked along, softly so that it didn't make a sound. One of them swung open, revealing darkness beyond. She leaned in, then pulled back and gave me a slightly shocked look before switching on the light inside.

The room was a very messy office. Boxes had been dumped haphazardly and a computer was half set up on the desk. A picture of Aline as a child was propped up beside it.

"Denise's stuff," said Amy. She pointed to a strange diagram of circles and arrows on a whiteboard. "Something about how the demons get out of the realm without using the portal. Looks like there's a schematic of that..." She pointed to a dark box in the corner.

It was about half as tall as an old-fashioned telephone booth (I'd seen those on TV) and was open on one side. It didn't appear to have anything in it, but I felt drawn to it. My skin tingled and I was reminded of iron filings standing up when a magnet was waved over them. It was as if those iron filings were in my blood and that box was the magnet. I rubbed my arms.

"So you feel it too?" asked Amy.

"I... I guess."

"This may sound crazy, but I want to examine everything in this room and get as much information as we can, and then we can go look at whatever that is."

"Uh... nothing's crazy at this point. That sounds good," I said.

Part 3:

Liana

THIRTY

Even as I panicked, I had to hug my friends, which was no easy feat in the pitch dark. Elbows hit eyes and fingers snagged on and pulled hair. It didn't matter, though; we figured out how to wrap our arms around each other and hold tight.

Much like when I'd first held Corban in the waiting room, I knew that my friends were truly here, because they were solid and real. Their hair smelled freshly washed and their skin clean.

I no doubt reeked in contrast, but they didn't seem to care.

"Where are we?" Amy kept asking.

"Yeah it's the demon realm," said Corban, his hand still clasping my shoulder. "Guys, why are you here?"

"How are you here?" I asked.

"We think it's the ferrum in our blood," said Amy. "And Denise had this ma—"

"Shhh," said Corban. "We aren't alone."

Gamlat chuckled.

My friends went silent and I hugged them tighter.

"Who is that?" Gina whispered to me.

But it was Gamlat who answered, with questions of her own. "She did what now? And who, pray tell, is Denise?"

Amy and Gina dug their fingers into my arms, heedless of any bruises they would leave.

"Sorry," I whispered to them. "That's Gamlat. The human. The host. Not the demon."

"So you are here," said Amy. "Did you turn out the lights?"

Gamlat laughed. "Ah, did I? I don't know. I suppose that depends on how you look at things. Would you like them turned back on?"

"Yes?" Gina ventured.

I expected Gamlat to laugh, but for several seconds, nothing happened. My friends' breathing rasped and my heart thundered in the silence.

"Stars," said Amy.

I looked up, and sure enough, some stars were peeking through the inky blackness.

"She's abandoning us," said Corban. "We need to stay in this darkness if we want to avoid being found by Xiii."

"Who's that?" asked Gina.

No matter which direction we looked, though, the cloud was thinning. Corban's pale form took shape, so I could see him darting this way and that, nervous about being exposed once the darkness was gone entirely.

Amy and Gina's forms became clear, too, and Amy was the first to let go and step back.

We were on the endless black plain, too exposed, with a line of white demarcating the horizon and scattered dots of light below it and stars above. All shelter was remote—strange, boxy compounds, fifty yards away at least—and those compounds didn't look much like shelter because they glowed.

As did we. Our skin had a slight luminescence to it, not as bright as the other demons—which I thought only made us stand out more.

So my stomach churned like a rock tumbler as I, like Corban, scanned the area for a place to hide.

Amy got out her little portable data drive and tapped the screen. At least Gina was content to keep clinging to me.

"Aline said the beings here lived in huts," I said. "Those are not huts."

"Gamlat's been here, other humans have been here," said Corban. "They taught the inhabitants a thing or two.

Amy kept tapping away.

"What are you doing?" I asked her.

Corban's stance indicated that he could move at a split-second's notice. He had enough fighting experience that I trusted him to spot danger if it came towards us. "The moon's down," he said.

"What?" I asked.

"The moon." He looked at me. "I saw it rise. Now it's down again."

Amy still hadn't answered me and my temper was so frayed that I was on the verge of snapping at her.

"We can maybe find shelter at the human village," she finally said.

"What human village?" I asked.

"Back when people used to export a lot of ferrum out of this realm, there was a permanent human village. I've got a map for how to find it using the stars." She held up the phone to the sky and squinted at it, turning slowly. "There was an app we downloaded from Denise's computer. Seems to work on this drive... I need to find the pole star."

"The humans have all been expelled from here," I said. "And... how did you get to Denise's computer?"

"Long story," said Amy. "We can tell it on the way to the village, which is in a cave and should provide cover."

"Do we even know if it still exists?" I asked. "And if it does, it seems like a really obvious place for us to go. Xiii will find us there."

"Well, that's the thing about this realm. According to the notes the coyote-shifters have, the inhabitants don't know how to navigate. They remember the places they visit often, and are able to keep finding them with the shifting around that happens if they travel the routes often enough to keep up. Places they haven't been for a while, they often can't find again. The portal is the one thing everyone can always find."

"Sooo," I said. "Even if you have a map to this village, it will have moved."

"It won't."

"But things are always shifting around."

"Except that you can still navigate," she replied. "I do not understand how it works, but humans lived and worked here for centuries and the coyote-shifters navigated them around."

Corban looked back and forth between us and shrugged. "Maybe the human village is like the pole star? Maybe it stays put?"

My head ached. "How far do we have to walk to get to this village?" I asked. "It could be a million miles away."

"Well, distances aren't fixed here. It doesn't take very long to get anywhere."

That made even less sense, but given Amy was the one person with confidence and a plan, I figured I'd go along with it. When she started to walk, Gina and I followed. Corban brought up the rear, his gaze still scanning the horizon.

Gina hitched her sweatshirt more tightly around herself, even though it wasn't cold. I understood, though. The place felt like it ought to be cold. It was so empty and sterile and unreal. Our footfalls were silent, and there wasn't even the soft sound of rustling clothes as we moved.

"So... we should catch each other up," I said. "Explain how we all got here. You guys first."

Gina told her story, finishing with, "I don't know if the coyote-shifters will be mad at us or what. We just... we felt like we needed to gather as much information as we could from Denise's office, and then we went to look at her machine and... kind of fell through it. The ferrum in our blood pulled us through the border between realms, but it's apparently a one-way thing."

"Does that data drive have any advice on how to close the portal?" I asked.

"No," said Amy. "That's what Denise was obsessed with, and she couldn't divine any answers."

Corban snorted at her choice of words. "Maybe the divine powers-that-be are withholding all answers."

His joke bothered me. It sounded too similar to what Gamlat had said about the powers-that-be.

Besides, I felt responsible for my two best friends being trapped here. No, I was responsible. It would have been far kinder for me to refuse their friendship years ago, when I first knew I was a vampire. I'd endangered them that whole time; what if I'd turned while I was with them? I nearly had once when I was getting a ride home with Gina.

What kind of ridiculous, selfish person did that?

Gina rammed me with her shoulder, not hard enough to knock me over, but I still stumbled several steps. "Spill," she ordered me. "What dark thoughts are you thinking?"

"That we're all going to die here and it's my fault."

"Why? Because your destiny brought you here?" she asked. "So did ours. Don't make this all about you."

"Yeah," Amy chimed in. "This is our adventure, too."

"Guys," I said.

"Tell us what's happened to you," said Gina. "How'd you end up in that dark cloud?"

I told them as we trudged along the plain.

I felt like we were bugs on a plate glass window, liable to slip off into oblivion at any moment. But I didn't, nor did my friends.

We kept on trudging along, passing various ghostly compounds that were silent sentinels on our path.

"So..." said Gina once I finished, "I am definitely for finding the third Nabatean vampire and killing her."

"You okay with doing Satan's will at the same time?" Corban asked.

"That's the kicker," Gina agreed.

"I should have asked Gamlat why she didn't do it herself," I said. "I didn't realize she'd poof like that."

"There!" said Amy, pointing.

At first it didn't look like she was pointing at anything but a patch of darkness. Then I noticed a soft glow, not as vivid as the dwellings scattered around on the plain.

As we drew closer, my brain slowly made sense of what I saw. There was a hill in front of us with a cave in the side. All of the glow emanated from the cave, and as we got closer, I saw that the entire inside of the cave was decorated with softly glowing murals. A seascape took up one wall with waves crashing against cliffs. A jungle scene took up another with tree trunks and dark shadows and an expanse of leafy greenery at the top. A jaguar was slinking out from the shadows, its eyes sparkling with faceted jewels.

We were close enough now that I could see that these murals were tiled, not painted, and the ceiling of the cave was shaded dark blue in the back and light blue towards the cave's mouth. A brilliant sun dominated the light blue, a moon the middle section, and only stars at the back.

Nestled in the cave were dwellings. They looked a bit like the cliff dwellings that some Native Americans in New Mexico had lived in: boxy, earthen, and built up against the walls of the cave.

They also looked deserted. Gina put two fingers in her mouth and let out a piercing whistle.

"Hello?" she yelled. "Anybody home?"

THIRTY-ONE

G ina's words echoed hollowly in the great expanse of the cavern. Now that we stood at its mouth, I saw that the uneven rock floor was littered with debris. Potshards and splintered, wooden remains of benches and tables painted a picture of a violent expulsion. This place had been looted, probably when the inhabitants were evicted. All that remained was the smell of cold stone, dust, and ancient secrets.

"Wow..." Amy whispered. She was staring at the tiled jaguar, its red-gemmed eyes glinting at us. "This is... a couple thousand years old at least?"

"The ferrum exports wrapped up around the same time as my ascent," Corban confirmed. "So yeah, probably something like that."

She picked her way forward across the junk-strewn floor, then looked back at us. "Okay if I look around?"

"Um, not alone," said Gina.

I agreed, and the two of us headed after her.

Corban, again, stayed at the back of the group, looking around, assessing threats.

So far, I'd seen no sign that anyone was following us, but the only sign I knew to look out for was people, literally, following us. He probably could do better than that, and that provided some relief against the existential stress of the situation.

Amy paused to look at a broken chair. "Wood, cloth. No leather. The cloth doesn't bleach or biodegrade here. Weird."

I had to agree, and since she'd brought up biodegradation, I was curious now too. The cloth of the chair was ripped and wrinkled, but it still looked new, as if this breakage had occurred yesterday. It was a simple, rough weave.

Gina picked up a pot shard and examined it. "It's decorated, with paint. I'm guessing that the humans decorated it, 'cause it's a little asymmetrical. Like someone did this by hand." The piece she held was pale clay painted blue and red.

Amy, I noticed, did not look at it. Her beloved, Jack, was a potter, and now didn't seem like the time to try to break through her ironclad reserve and ask about him.

"Not sure what day-to-day life was like here," said Amy. "They actually mined some of the ferrum out of the back of the cave and traded the demons for the rest of it. Cartloads were hauled to the ziggurat and then carried on up to the portal."

"Who were the people who were here?" I asked. "Nabateans?"

"Some of them, in the later years. There were some Persians as well. Everyone relied on the coyote-shifters, and the angelic order bought all the ferrum. I guess there was some arms-length provision to keep the order from finding out too many specifics about the coyote-shifters. And I guess the coyote-shifters were in it for the vast sums of money it brought them."

Corban looked around and shook his head. "Unreal." He picked up another pot shard and squinted at it.

Gina had put her shard down, though, and was rubbing her arms. "Something feels wrong about this place."

"Well, sure," said Amy. "It's an abandoned human village in the demon realm."

"There's no sound," I pointed out, pushing at some wood planks with my toe. Rather than scraping against the ground, there was only silence.

"No..." said Gina. "I feel like we're being watched."

I took a good look at the dwellings, the closest of which were still a good twenty yards away, up stairs that had been carved into the rock floor. "People were clearly thrown out of this place," I said, gesturing at all the debris on the floor. "Doesn't leave warm, fuzzy feelings behind."

"That's not it," Gina insisted.

Corban nodded. "Yeah, I feel it too. Like someone's staring at my back, but the feeling doesn't go away when I turn around."

I could believe Gina was paranoid (I was too), but Corban had too much experience for me to dismiss. A shiver passed over my skin and I found myself rubbing my arms the same way Gina had. "What do you think it is?"

"I can search the buildings," Corban offered.

"Be honest," I said. "Is that a good idea?"

"If there's a group in one of them, I could get overpowered..."

"Don't endanger yourself," I told Corban. Then I turned to Amy and asked, "Did the humans have any other friends or allies here?"

"Regular trading partners, probably," said Amy. "I don't have a list of names or addresses, though."

"Helloooo!" Gina called out again. "Is anybody here?"

Again, there was only silence, but given how nothing here other than speech and breath and heartbeats made noise, I realized there could be thousands of demons packed into those dwellings and I'd have no idea.

No, I told myself. They glow. I'd see the glow.

"Let's all look in there," Gina pointed at the nearest dwelling. "I gotta do something. I'm going to lose my mind."

"Stay behind me," said Corban. He strode soundlessly to the front of the group and started on up the stairs. He didn't do anything to conceal his approach, I noticed. He even whistled a tune to give anyone inside fair warning.

Gina and I climbed the steps, holding hands. My back itched, like someone was pressing the blade of a dagger to my skin.

"Anyone here?" Corban called out, knocking on the empty frame of the door. Then he said something else, which I assumed were the same words in Arabic or Persian... no, Farsi. That was the Persian language. I wondered if the translations were necessary. The demons seemed to understand English just fine, and I doubted Gamlat had taught them all.

Though Corban moved as if he was at ease, I saw the telltale signs that he wasn't: the tension in his back muscles, the way he kept his weight low and kept turning his head to see as much as he could.

Now he'd gone completely rigid. "Show yourself!" he demanded, cycling through some other languages.

Gina clamped onto one of my arms and Amy the other. I was beyond grateful to have them there, but not thrilled that this meant they were also in danger.

"Hands up!" Corban ordered.

Inside the dwelling a light appeared, transitioning the interior from impenetrable blackness to dimly illuminated walls and beamed ceiling. Again, I was reminded of puebloan architecture in New Mexico.

A woman stepped into view, her face framed by the window, and I felt a scream rising in my throat.

It was Saf. Her visage had been burned into my memory by the vision I'd seen of her. Her black eyes took in our group.

"Fools," she said. "You brought them here."

I looked at my friends, both of whom had gone rigid with fright.

"Not them," said Saf. She nodded at something behind me. "Them. Why do you think they let you go? Probably so you could find me for them."

Both of my friends turned, but I didn't want to let Saf out of my line of sight. Odds were, she was trying to make us look away so she could pounce.

But my friends both clamped down tighter on my, now sore, arms. There was definitely something there.

Corban had glanced back once, and now turned around, his face grim.

"You brought him right to me," Saf shrieked. "Like idiots."

I made myself look back and saw nothing but darkness. Which was a problem, because I should have seen stars, the white line of the horizon, and the scattered dots of nearer compounds.

I tore my gaze away from this and back to Saf, only to find her right in front of me. Her cruel smile filled my field of vision as her hand closed around my throat, causing pressure, but no other sensation. I didn't feel icy fingers or a tensing of muscles under skin, only the constriction around my neck. Panic rose in my chest.

Corban clubbed her on the shoulder with a plank of wood, knocking her back, but she was laughing. "Such primitives."

She grabbed the wooden plank and jerked it out of Corban's grip. He let it go and backed away to avoid her swing. I tried to back away too, and stumbled backwards down the stairs, taking my friends with me. My heart raced as my mind grappled with the sensation of taking a step and finding the ground several inches lower than I'd expected.

Amy let go, but Gina clung tighter and we both went down. My foot went through the fabric of a broken chair, and even this did not produce any sound. Nor did my body smacking into the floor. I felt it happen, but without hearing it, it didn't seem real. Corban grunted as he dodged Saf's swing.

There was no mistaking it now, though, the darkness was entering the cave, inky tendrils flowing along the walls like a giant octopus reaching in to grab its prey.

I got up onto my knees in time to see Saf wave her hand and the light in the cave went bright and orange. Amy clapped her hands over her mouth, eyes wide with fear. I turned to see that there was a wall of fire at the mouth of the cave.

"We have to get out!" Corban shouted. "Before it eats all the oxygen."

Saf burst out laughing. "You still think you're on Earth. Nobody dies here, though yes, this is a very effective way to get rid of a lot of people at once there. A technique I invented, I believe. Quite useful, I must say."

My vision was graying out as the air grew more thin. Corban's shouts sounded distant, and muted.

THIRTY-TWO

I must have blacked out. When I came to, someone was prodding me to get up. I startled and sat up, my head spinning and the world tilting so violently that I nearly threw up.

"Liana, it's me." Corban's voice.

There was a strong wind that whipped my hair and plastered my clothes to my body. It was like being in a storm, without the moisture or cold. There was sound, though. The wind roared, not quite as loud as I was used to, but at least the infernal silence was gone.

We were still in the cavern, and Corban was trying to drag me towards the stairs. A glance over my shoulder revealed the fire was gone, replaced by a swarm of winged demons, so many that they formed a wall of flapping wings and flowing robes. They were taking turns diving into the cave and getting blown back.

A tiny cluster of figures at the top of the stairs were what held them off. Saf stood at the center, but they all waved their hands and hurled the great gusts of wind. She hadn't been alone in here.

"Come on," Corban shouted over the roar of rushing air. "They'll figure out walking works better than flying any minute."

I got to my feet and pushed forward against the headwind, demonstrating to everyone behind us that this was how to get into the cave. I felt, more than saw, the winged demons behind us landing, their glow consolidating along the ground as they formed up ranks and tried to march.

The wind abated and I stumbled forward, adjusting for the lack of resistance. Corban hauled me forward at a run, his fist gripping my forearm painfully as we made for the small cluster of demons trying to hold the cave.

We reached them and I turned just as fire leapt up across the mouth of the cave again, a great wall of it that crackled and roared and was blistering hot.

"Wait," shouted Corban. "This is going to be worse now that the moon is up."

Saf shook her head, as if amused. "I'm not here to protect you," she said. "You chose to come here."

I cast about, looking for my friends and spotted them peering out the window of the nearest dwelling. They were safe, for now at least. Amy made eye contact with me and flashed a thumbs up.

"Liana, move," Corban ordered me.

A cloud of sparks filled the cave. The demons had begun to pour through the flames, heedless of how it set their robes alight. They came at us like mobile effigies. One, with a wave of a hand, extinguished the flames and restored his clothing—Ro, I now saw. He still wore his jeans and came at us with a look of deadly determination.

I made a beeline for my friends, ducked through the broken door, and skidded to a stop. They both grabbed me in a half-embrace, half-braking-maneuver. Once I had an arm around each of them, I felt a million times better, despite the warzone outside.

The inside of the dwelling was dim, save for the firelight flickering along the walls, making our shadows leap and dance.

"You guys okay?" I asked.

My friends pulled me down so that I sat with them on the floor, which was tiled and surprisingly clean. I would have expected a thick layer of dust, but there was none. This seemed as good a place as any to wait until the demons found us and did whatever it was they planned to do with us.

My vision was graying out again and my head tipped forward. The scent of char was in the air.

"Liana," said Amy, "the air isn't actually thinning here. Something about it not actually being air or... I don't know. Anyway, Saf thought it was hilarious to watch you pass out."

"But you guys didn't?" I asked.

"I almost did, but then I prayed to be able to breathe, and Saf thought that was hilarious too," said Gina.

"And I was too busy being creeped out by Saf," said Amy. "She is definitely a demon."

Corban came charging into the room. "We gotta go," he said. "There's a passage. We gotta take the passage."

I looked out the window and saw the darkness pouring into the cave once more, extinguishing the flames and enveloping the first line of demons who had broken through. From their confident stances, it was clear that they were either controlling the darkness, or trusted whoever did. Saf's great gusts of wind and gouts of flame did little against it. They would have her captured in short order.

"Follow me!" Corban whisper-shouted. He grabbed my wrist and I took Gina's hand.

"Everyone hold hands," I ordered, also at a whisper.

Gina took Amy's hand. We were all linked up now, a human chain. Without the fire, the light was dimmer, but still bright enough that I could see everyone clearly.

"You will not win this!" screamed Saf.

That was the last I heard before Corban hauled me through a doorway—that I didn't see until I stepped through it—and to some stairs that I nearly fell down.

"What is this?" I asked.

"A secret passage. Uses an optical illusion that I don't have time to explain. Let's go."

We were in a tunnel now, and it was getting darker and darker, the farther we moved from the door and stairs. I expected the scent of dank, cold stone, but it was very faint, as if whatever force that gave life to the flames and wind didn't reach back here.

Soon we were feeling our way along in pitch darkness. When Corban finally stopped, I ran right into him.

"So... it's done," I said. "They have her and they'll close the portal." And they'd capture us and force us out. This was not the ending I'd hoped for, but perhaps it was the ending that was meant to be. I wasn't sure what else we could do right now.

As if to mock me, there came a shockwave through the floor and walls that almost knocked us off our feet. I was thrown against the wall and if I'd dropped Gina or Corban's hand, I could have braced for impact.

There was no way I was letting go of either of them.

"They don't have her yet," said Corban.

"Where does this tunnel lead?" I asked.

"Why aren't we helping them catch Saf?" That was Amy.

"I agree," said Gina. "If that is Saf, then I agree with Gamlat. Xiii's not evil. He's trying to save his people."

"Whoa, whoa, whoa," Corban argued. "Hang on a minute. Saf's the key to this world finishing its creation according to the plan."

"That is definitely not our problem," said Gina.

Since I knew where the wall was, I moved over to lean against it, still clutching my friends' hands. "Corban," I said, "maybe this is how it's supposed to go. We found her for them, and she has done terrible things on Earth."

"I know."

"She used to herd people into caves and light fires at the mouth to suffocate them all. She says she invented that."

"Oh, no way," said Amy. "Seriously?"

"Is that extra bad or something?" Gina demanded. "I mean is it worse than it sounds? Because it does sound bad."

"It's a primitive form of gas chamber," said Amy. "It probably inspired later inventions like gas chambers. Think of all the evil that has been done with gas chambers. They're synonymous with ethnic cleansing and holocausts."

"She's evil," I agreed. "She'd totally bite the apple if she went to their Garden of Eden. If we let things play out, maybe we really are doing the right thing."

"We can't pretend we're passive observers here," said Corban. "Because we led Xiii right to her. Nobody knew how to find he—"

"Before I showed up with a map?" said Amy. "I'm okay with that. Call me complicit, I don't care."

Corban put a hand on my shoulder and I sensed he was trying to look me in the eye. It was too dark for that to be possible, though. "Remember how confusing things were when we met the angel and then Xiii? We've got to think hard about this because sometimes the answer isn't obvious. If a messenger from the creator said we need to rescue Saf, we need to think hard about this."

"I know, but is that what the creator wanted us to do?" I asked. "And I'm having trouble getting past the whole gas chamber thing. Call me distractible, but..."

"No... wait," said Gina. She knocked her head softly against the wall and muttered something. Then she said, "Saf is from here originally, right? She brought the idea of suffocating people to Earth, not the other way around."

"She figured it out on Earth because Earth is an evil place," I explained. "With air. You can do what she did there, here."

"But... no. Think about how all vampires and fallen angels and plague-scourge demons are on Earth," said Gina. "They start doing evil the moment they show up."

"And Earth is not an... inherently evil place," Amy conceded. "Liana, you are a good person. You protected us from the demon inside you. If you hadn't, my brother would be dead."

"You gave me a place to live when my family threw me out," said Gina.

"Evil things happen on Earth," I said, directing my words towards Amy. "Look at how your ancestors were treated, and how your people are still treated."

"Agreed," said Corban, "and I can fill in a few thousand more examples from my own personal experience, if you like. That being said—"

"I can't believe I'm about to say this," Amy cut him off, "but as awful as history has been for us, it could have been worse. Getting devoured by demons would have been worse. Half-turned demons have used human morality to keep humanity safe from the worst for millennia. It's something only humans can do. Gina's got a point."

"We know there's good on Earth too," I said. "It started out as good."

Gina let go of my hand and pulled out her cell phone. "Hang on, I'm having a thought here."

THIRTY-THREE

"Genesis Three," said Gina, tapping on her phone screen. "The forbidden fruit in the garden didn't introduce evil. Satan was already in the garden at that point. The fruit gave Eve the knowledge of good and evil. The beings here lack the knowledge. Interesting that they pretty much always choose to do evil."

"Fair point," said Corban.

Yes, it was. And I'd known the words of the scripture, I just hadn't considered them before. "Is that an accurate translation?" I asked him.

He shut his eyes a moment. I could only just make out his features by the light of the cell phone screen. His lips moved as he went through his memories of languages long dead. "Yeah... it is. For these purposes."

"Okay, so wait," said Amy. "There's something else I need to point out. Humanity's had a few watershed moments in its evolutionary history."

"Though, are we going with Christianity or evolution?" Gina challenged.

"No," I said. "Let's not get into that debate right now. What were you going to say, Amy?"

"We don't know much about the first tamer of demons," said Amy. "But we know the chronology of the second. Otuo founded the angelic order at roughly the same time as the prehistoric cognitive revolution."

"What was that?" I asked.

"Humanity was in the Stone Age for over a hundred thousand years, and then a few thousand years ago, we started developing more advanced technologies that have taken us from stone tools to supercomputers in a tiny fraction of the time it took us to go from spears to arrows. That began, some people think, with the development of abstract concepts."

"No, I know this," said Corban, excitement building in his voice. "Humans already had the capacity to understand right and wrong, but Otuo put it to practical use. He showed how doing the right thing could have tangible benefits, as in, your body doesn't get used as an instrument of evil for eternity."

"Which enabled humans to start doing other stuff," said Amy. "Abstract concepts are what make us what we are. The idea of government is abstract, as is religion, mathematics, economics... All of those require conceptualizing an abstract idea or set of ideas and then acting in accordance to that abstract framework."

"You lost me," said Gina.

"Me too," said Corban.

She hadn't lost me. The pieces of the puzzle were coming together in my mind. "Money," I said, "is an abstract concept. The paper sheets we use have value because we all agree they have value. If I give you a dollar, we're agreeing that wealth has been transferred, but there's nothing practical behind that. If we got conquered by aliens tomorrow, we couldn't buy them off with money unless we got them to join our beliefs about money and participate in our rituals of trading paper for other things we need."

"Right... okay," said Gina.

"I kind of get that..." said Corban.

"So, like, justice," said Gina, "is abstract? Hitting someone over the head and taking their stuff is practically a good idea if there's no one to stop you, but all of us started believing it's bad and that's let us achieve something higher? We can cooperate to build cities and economies and judicial systems? While demons just run around hitting people over the head and taking their stuff?"

"Yes, okay, right," said Corban. "It's something Siobhan tried to explain to me right before we killed Melanie."

I grabbed the phone from Gina. "The Garden of Eden is about the first moral act," I said. "I mean, whether it was biting an apple or opening a portal... That's not necessarily the point. It's what the act meant that makes it significant."

"That first tamer of demons," said Amy, "probably got tricked somehow. But the result made Otuo's contribution to humanity possible. I mean... I guess history doesn't remember that first tamer."

"Nobody does," said Corban. "Even if the demons here all remember it, they won't understand it in those terms. Notice that everyone here can conjure, but they don't know how to close a portal. They've been here for who knows how many thousands of years, undying, able to learn over vast periods of time, and everything here is a pale reflection of stuff you find on Earth. There's no art or music or government or even a book club."

"Except in this cave," said Amy. "Where there is art. Where people put a ton of work into the art, even while here for other reasons. They couldn't conjure, so they must've traded for or brought in the materials—which wasn't easy. But it's totally human. Lemme tell ya, there are archeological sites all over Earth were people did insanely complicated things to make their surroundings beautiful, or appealing to their gods, or to represent concepts that they revered, or remember ancestors they loved. It's something we can all relate to."

Gina nodded. "Yeah... so... I was trying to say that Earth isn't an evil place because people from Earth aren't evil—not all of them at least. A lot of them are good."

"So, taking your point about Genesis," I said, "people have the power to choose to be good because we've all bitten the proverbial apple. That comes at a really high price, though. Think of all the people on Earth who suffer because they know what's right and that isn't what they're given. Would it really be worse for them not to know? I mean, assuming we can actually do anything about this, is it really up to a bunch of people from the richest country on Earth to tell the demon realm that they should live like we do? We're all winners in that system, some of us more than others, but still. I believe that gets worked out in an afterlife, but…"

"My people are not winners in that system," Amy snapped, her vehemence taking me aback.

I knew about oppression against Native Americans, of course, but Amy didn't talk about it much. I'd been to her house, which had been inherited down through the generations. Her people had been the first farmers in the region and built the first cities, but now many of them lived in poverty. Her home had been rich in tradition and love, but poor in material goods. Whereas I was rich, with a house on land taken from the indigenous peoples, and a body nourished by foods that had originally been cultivated by them, and a fortune that my family has amassed over generations when no one else had been invading our space or taking our things.

"It's not a great choice," Amy went on, "but I'd rather be tormented by people with a theory about why what they do is right than by beings who don't even think about it. You can argue with the first group. The US has tortured my people and stolen land from us and broken up our families and involuntarily sterilized us and manages us with the same government department that manages wildlife."

I winced. Everything she said was true.

"But," she went on, "my mom is a state senator and my brother was proud to serve in the Army, because the ideals are there even if the execution is… lacking. He loves the USA and is fanatical about flying the flag. I'm not there yet, but I do get his point. He does have a point. I was able to get a first class education where I can start shaping some of the research on indigenous peoples. There's a way forward sometimes when you deal with humans. That's not how things work with demons."

"Okay, and I agree with all that," said Gina. She spoke slowly, as if expecting Amy to lash out at her. "I think maybe the other thing to think about is that people here have no choice. Not about anything that matters."

"They all have mansions, it looks like," I said.

"You have a mansion," said Corban. "Does that automatically make you happy?"

"Ask someone without a mansion," I countered. "I think they might have an opinion about that."

"No, guys." Gina was annoyed. "If people here can't choose whether to be good or bad, Xiii is choosing for them. He's taking the choice away. His act is the only act that has moral significance and he's not choosing to banish evil. He's choosing to keep everyone ignorant of it. That's bad."

"Here! There's a door here!" shouted a voice. "They're hiding in there."

"Where does this passage lead?" I asked Corban.

"Nowhere," he said. "It dead ends here."

Gina held up her phone to reveal a rugged wall. "This was either a ferrum mine, though I don't know what that would look like, or a hidey-hole."

"And now it's neither," said Corban.

I could hear soft footfalls echoing down the corridor as our captors piled on in.

"I can fight them off for a while," said Corban. "None of them know how to fight back."

"Oh, is that so?" Ro rounded the bend and stood with his hands on his hips. He had wings now, which he kept folded in the narrow space. The light of his figure illuminated our little band. "I mean... you have had about nineteen years more training than I have, so what do I know? Oh, and I have a dozen guys who know enough basics to take care of these girls, here. You aren't the first humans, with your warlike ways, to spend time in this realm."

Corban dropped into fighting stance.

"No," I said. It didn't make logical sense to fight a battle we were sure to lose. We couldn't do anything to affect Saf if we were duking it out in here. "We get captured, okay? That's what we do."

Much to my surprise, my friends obeyed. Corban stood up straighter and held up his hands. I'd thought I'd known fear before now. Being almost killed by vampires was nothing compared to having the people I loved most in the world trust me with the fate of their souls, though.

I took a deep breath and tried to calm my terror.

THIRTY-FOUR

Ro led us back out of the tunnel and into the main cavern, which now smelled like ozone and ash. There were scorch marks on the floor and charring on the beautiful murals.

A small, slender woman had pinned Saf down a few yards beyond the base of the stairs. There was no sign of the demons who'd fought beside Saf. "Strips of cloth," the woman was shouting. "I can tie her so that it won't matter that she can conjure a knife. Conjure me cloth, or just rip some strips off that chair!"

"Ah, the skills one learns on Earth," said Corban.

"That's Gamlat," I realized. Then I felt stupid. Of course it was. She was wearing a plain dress rather than robes, and didn't have the black, demonic eyes.

Now that I could see her, I was surprised at how slight she was, though I shouldn't have been. Otuo had also been very short; those two were so old that they predated all the modern races. Like Otuo, she had dark skin, but hers was more reddish, as was her kinked hair. Her eyes, I suspected, were gray rather than brown. I couldn't see from this distance.

Beyond the cave, the blackness still roiled, like a baleful cloud of ink ready to smother anything that crossed it.

Saf screamed.

"Yes, that's pain. You remember pain, surely?" said the woman with a chuckle.

Xiii stepped out of the roiling darkness and surveyed the scene. "Ah, you found them!" he called out to Ro. His gaze fell on Gina and Amy and his eyebrows shot up. "Who are you?"

Neither of my friends replied, whether out of prudence or fear, I couldn't say. Either served at a time like this.

"Lock them up somewhere where they won't interfere," said Xiii to Ro. "It shouldn't take long to find the other dissidents."

My ears pricked up at that. My decision not to put up a fight hadn't been in vain? They needed to find the other dissidents? That meant there was time between now and Saf's exile and death. There had to be a way to make use of that. "Saf!" I called out.

Ro clubbed me on the side of the head, hard enough that my ear rang. "Quiet," he ordered me.

How on Earth was I going to talk to her?

Gamlat, who had managed to acquire some cloth and tie Saf up, got to her feet and bowed to Xiii. "If you will permit me to go through the portal, I will kill her for you."

Xiii frowned, then looked at us.

Gina stepped forward. "You need someone to kill Saf on the other side of the portal, did I hear you say? Sign me up!" She looked sidelong at me, eyes pleading.

Oh... I paused a minute, hoping that I was not misreading the situation, then reared back and slapped her, hard as I could.

Gina recoiled, then spat in my face.

Gross. I wiped it away with my sleeve.

Corban moved so fast he was a blur, shoving Gina back and inserting himself between us, arms extended, palms out, signaling that he would not tolerate us going after each other.

Physically, at least. "You can't kill Saf," I shouted at Gina. "You're playing right into Satan's hands. Corban, get out of the way!"

"And you're so blind you don't understand right from wrong. You'll follow a side based on what they look like and who they say they are, not who they show themselves to be," she retorted.

"Now, now, ladies," said Xiii. "Don't fight."

"Guys," said Amy. "Gina's right. Liana, seriously, you don't have to do this. We'll do it. You're off the hook. Leave it alone."

"I have to stop you," I said.

"Okay, if this is because you believe martyring yourself is the way out of any difficult situation," said Amy, "that's idiotic. I'm just saying. That part of Christianity is stupid."

"Amy." There was a warning note in Corban's voice. "You don't have to believe as we do, but a little respect, please?"

"Shut up," I told Corban, shoving him ineffectually. "Get out of the way!"

"Yeah, I thought this situation was kind of important," Amy retorted. "I'm sorry if I'm being uncivil while discussing the potential end of human civilization. Gee, what was I thinking?"

Corban's jaw clenched so hard that his cheek muscles flexed. He took a deep breath, holding himself back from leaping at her and grabbing her by the throat.

"I will kill Saf," said Gamlat, her voice sounding pathetic and frail after all of our shouting. "I have been waiting for who knows how long for the opportunity? I was the one who tracked these four right to her."

"Uh, and we were the ones who found her," said Gina.

"Tie all of them up," said Xiii.

Ro grabbed a nearby chair, ripped loose some strips of cloth, and dove at Corban.

This was going to be a long fight. These two had shared a body and a training regimen for two thousand years.

But Corban ducked aside and said, "Tie her up first, and the rest of us will go peacefully." He pointed at Gina.

Ro kept an eye on Corban, stepping carefully around with his gaze fixed on Corban's hands. Corban kept them visible, so Ro glanced away long enough to truss Gina up. Then he tied up Amy, then he nodded towards me.

Corban pointed at Gamlat, whose eyes widened with fury. "I will not be treated like the enemy in this!"

"Uh, if you are the enemy, they're gonna treat you like one," he answered.

"I will kill Saf!" Gamlat declared.

"Suuuure you will." He shook his head. "You spent how many thousands of years as a guardian angel? I'm sure they'll totally trust you."

Saf, who had been laying on her side with her back to us, sighed in real frustration. "Send me through the portal with all of the ones who say they want to kill me and I'm sure one of them will get it done."

Ro spread his wings, launched himself into the air, and dove at Gamlat. She misjudged his fighting skills, clearly expecting an inexperienced demon. A split second's hesitation was all it took for Ro to overpower her, and soon she, too, was tied up.

One of the other demons handed him more strips of cloth and he turned back to Corban, one eyebrow lifted in query.

"Fine," said Corban. He put his hands behind his back and let Ro tie him up.

Someone came up behind me, startling me when she stepped into my peripheral vision. Jaelyn. I let her tie me up, wincing as she pulled the bonds tight. I wondered if I could lose body parts here. Perhaps I couldn't die, but could still lose my hands if the circulation was cut off too long. Jaelyn and Ro made us all sit down on the hard cave floor. I'd felt powerless this entire time, but now I felt even more so.

"All right," said Xiii. "We have four dissidents to find."

What? They'd promised to lock us up. We needed to all get locked up together. I rolled over and aimed a two-footed kick at Gina, who squealed and tried to get away.

Amy, meanwhile, moved like an inchworm towards the stairs and Saf, a murderous look in her eyes.

"Perhaps we should give them some privacy to work this out," said Xiii. "Put them in there."

I couldn't see where he pointed, but demons scrambled to grab us and threw us over their shoulders. I nearly retched as my gut came into contact with an unyielding shoulder.

We were being carried to a nearby dwelling.

"We'll leave you to finish your conversations in peace," said Xiii.

Apparently irony was a live concept here.

I was flung to the ground hard enough that my head hit with a loud crack. It hurt, but stars didn't swim in my vision. Weird.

Gina was thrown down next to me and Saf on the other side. As I scrambled to sit up, Corban and Amy were both hurled in, hitting the floor and skidding.

Ouch, I thought.

Our captors covered the doorway and window with boards of wood—likely the remains of the original door and shutters. Saf's luminosity was plenty of light to see by, though.

"Can I expect you to faithfully guard them?" Xiii said outside.

"Yes, sir," said Ro.

"Absolutely." That was Jaelyn.

"Because if you don't, expect to be thrown through the portal as well."

"Of course," agreed Jaelyn. "I understand."

I prodded Gina with my toes.

"Quit it!" she yelled.

"Guys, I'm banishing you to corners," said Corban. "I'm not gonna put up with you guys fighting for who knows how long. Quiet!"

I let out a deep breath, then rolled over and sat up, grinning.

Gamlat groaned. "Oh please. No..."

We'd done it. We'd gotten ourselves locked up with Saf.

I ignored Gamlat, who sat in the shadows, as far away from Saf as possible.

"Okay, okay," I said.

My friends all levered themselves up to sitting position, grinning in triumph. Corban hesitated a minute, then began to chuckle.

"Nice," he said.

Saf let out a groan. "They were playing you!" she shouted. "They just wanted to be locked up together to plot some pathetic little scheme."

"Shut up, Saf," Ro replied.

"Aw," I said, "the problem with being the realm's least trusted person. Nobody will believe you when you try to tell on anyone else. What?" I said, raising my voice. "You don't want to be trapped here alone with us?"

"Okay, we don't know how much time we have," whispered Gina, in charge as always. "So let's talk."

"Right," whispered Amy. "So... how does this work?"

We all exchanged blank looks.

Gamlat rolled her eyes.

THIRTY-FIVE

"You're all fools, you know that, right?" snapped Gamlat.

"Yeah, probably," Amy agreed. That was fair, but right then, fair was downright harsh. She was the truth teller of the group, though. It was part of what I loved about her... most of the time.

"What do you want?" Saf demanded. I noticed that even she whispered now. She was complicit in this much, at least.

"You've gotta accept your role in the creation of this world," I said.

"I left this realm to get away from that," she answered. "I literally went to hell to avoid it."

O-kaaay, I thought. We had how many minutes to make this work? This was insane. I took a long, deep breath.

"So, that's the thing," I said. "This role you'd play as the first woman, it has to be someone who's willing to do what she thinks is right, regardless of what other people tell her she has to do."

"I'm not stupid," Saf replied, glaring around at us. "I know who Eve was in the Earth tradition. She disobeyed God and is the reason why your world is hell. You should just kill me to sever our worlds, but nooo... You want this realm to suffer as a petty revenge."

"This isn't about revenge," said Amy. "Even though your kind helped make our world more hellish."

"Don't... don't say that," I said.

This situation was so odd. Did someone from yet another realm have to debrief Eve before she set foot in the Garden? Did an encounter like this cause her to eat an apple or open a portal to this realm or whatever it was she did?

Gamlat's amused gaze made me re-evaluate. Her smile was smug. She was watching me fail and enjoying every second of it. Maybe this conversation wasn't really about convincing Saf. Maybe it was so that we finished examining the concepts for ourselves.

Here went nothing. "Well..." I said, "Eve didn't know right from wrong, and she decided to gain that knowledge, which is pretty central to being human, living by abstract conce—"

"She disobeyed God," Saf repeated, like I was a stubborn child refusing to learn. "That is the definition of this 'wrong' concept, is it not? Not that this ever made much sense on Earth. It's 'wrong' to hurt people because they don't like it. Because I wouldn't like it if it happened to me... even though it didn't happen to me and never would." She looked around at us as if this were an obvious, winning argument.

"Yeah..."

But Gina spoke up. "Obedience doesn't mean anything if you can't disobey. My father always tells me that I should be obedient like he was to his father, but my dad was terrified of his dad. That's not obedience. That's blind following. It's only obedience if it's an actual choice. My dad couldn't ever tell me why I shouldn't be a metalworker, because he never thought about it. I did think about it, and if we get through this, I will have helped to save the world. Eve gave us free will. She was the first person to prove that you don't have to do what God says. It's a choice. And she didn't know she was disobeying the greater good because she didn't know the difference between good and evil."

Go Gina, I thought.

"Look," said Amy. "It isn't just Christianity that has this belief about the giver of knowledge being misunderstood, or even considered evil. Pandora and her box and all that, you know?"

"The little girl who opens a box and lets all the evils of the world loose?" asked Saf. "You going to say it's all worth it because hope also got released? There's no need for hope if you don't have pain, suffering, and pestilences. Hope was a consolation prize."

"That isn't true," I said. "Hope got weaker for me when my father died. Pain drives it out; it doesn't create it."

"My kind don't need hope," said Saf. "We're immortal. We can have whatever we want. Your kind live such short, pointless lives."

"Your kind have the pointless lives," said Corban. "Admit it, you can see that much. People on Earth do a lot more with their mortal lives than anyone here has done with an immortal one."

I wondered if she'd dispute that.

"Enough of this," said Gamlat, "if none of the rest of you will talk sense, then I will." She'd propped herself against the wall and sat with her knees drawn up to her chest. "This woman is responsible for every single vampire that ever walked on Earth, and even if she didn't turn them all, she gladly would have if given the opportunity."

Saf looked at her, her expression bland. She made no effort to push back against what Gamlat said.

"She killed thousands of people, and enjoyed flaying them alive herself," Gamlat went on.

"She didn't know it was wrong," said Gina. "She didn't understand the pain it caused."

"Now there you are wrong!" Gamlat wasn't bothering to whisper now. "Naive, stupid fool."

"Hey," I said.

"You don't bother inflicting pain if you don't know what pain is," said Gamlat. "She did know that she would scream in agony if it was done to her, that's why she did it to other people, to torture them. To make them hurt and scream and beg for mercy, which she never gave them because she doesn't see the point of it. Logically, there isn't one."

"Quiet in there," Ro said from outside.

"She is not innocent," Gamlat went on, ignoring him. "She enjoyed hurting people. She loved the feeling of power it gave her. She loved the looks on their faces when they stared at her in terror because she knows what fear is. Being a passenger in her mind for centuries means I know what she's like. Liana, if she could have shot your father, she might have. But she would have preferred to torment him first. To peel his skin off, pull his nails from his fingers—"

"Stop," I said.

"You want her to get away with all the pain and suffering she caused?" Gamlat asked. "Because she's not sorry, and if she goes on to become a mortal, she'll forget her past life. She'll never be sorry. You want to forgive her for that and move on?"

Corban strained against his bonds, moving towards me in a feeble effort to reach out. I could sense his desire to put an arm around me and pillow my head on his chest. That would have been perfect right now, but we were both tied up and that wasn't going to happen.

I opened my mouth and no sound came out. My father's murder had been an act of pure evil, carried out by a being who thought my pain was amusing. There had been nothing Dad could have done to dodge the bullet that took his life, either. Darissa would have killed him no matter what, simply because he was my dad.

Senseless violence like that was part of the existential evil on Earth. It was like the background music that made horror films horrific and sad songs sad. It was the sort of heinous unfairness that made us thirst for fairness. We all struggled to tolerate it. Forgiving it was always a tall order.

Especially given the amusement dancing in Saf's eyes.

Gamlat was nodding as well. "Now you're actually thinking about this. Finally."

I hadn't forgiven Darissa. I'd killed her in cold blood. Nor had I forgiven Melanie, or Evan. I'd ended them. That had felt like the right thing to do.

No, it was the right thing to do. I'd prevented them from hurting others. There were no prisons that could hold them or systems to reform them. I'd benefitted thousands of people down through future generations by killing vampires. They were demons.

Forgiving people... well, I wasn't a hundred percent on understanding why I always had to do that.

Forgiving demons though? Was that really a requirement?

"Just kill me," said Saf. "Torture me if you want, but you risk me getting away. And let's be clear, if I get away, I will scourge your planet until the end of time. No one was more powerful than I was. I won't feel sorry, either, whatever that means."

"No one is more powerful?" said a masculine voice. "Truly?"

She frowned and turned towards a corner of the room that looked empty, as far as I could see. "Who are you?" she demanded.

"Someone who is present whenever two or three people are gathered in my name. In this case, four."

"Is that Biblical?" Amy demanded.

"Um... yeah..." I said. "It is."

THIRTY-SIX

But my friends were gone. Saf was gone. Our prison was gone.

Instead I found myself sitting, without bonds, on top of a small rise, a place I knew well. It was where I'd sat my first morning in New Mexico, waiting on the sunrise. Aunt Cassie's house was nearby, and desert stretched nearly as far as the eye could see. A jagged canyon cut through the middle distance, and mountains formed the boundary of the Taos Valley. They were tinged with blue, as if so far away that there was a little sky between me and them.

I heaved a deep breath and turned to the person I knew was sitting next to me, even though I'd neither seen nor heard him.

The man smiled back at me. I could see him there with even more certainty than I could place myself on this hill. That being said, I couldn't define anything about him. I couldn't have said what color his eyes were, or his hair, or his skin. I sensed he wore plain, rough-spun clothing, but couldn't have described it. He was like the language in the Starlight Kingdom, or the magazines in the waiting room. Again I considered Gamlat's idea that I was sitting with a human concept rather than reality.

But, I wasn't sure the distinction mattered anymore. As Gamlat theorized, people lived in a world of their own ideas. They were real enough to save or end us.

The man smiled, as if reading my thoughts and finding them amusing.

I waited for him to speak. That seemed appropriate.

"Quite some friends you chose," he said.

"They chose me," I replied. "They found me crying in the bathroom on my first day of school and kept on being nice to me."

He nodded, not disputing my point, and said nothing more.

I waited as the sun warmed my skin and the silence stretched on. In Taos, there wasn't much ambient noise. Right now there were no singing insects, no chirping birds, not even the whoosh of traffic on the highway. There was only the slight breath of breeze through the grass and the occasional buzz of a grasshopper hopping. Solitude reigned supreme.

It was my turn to speak, then. "You're going to tell me to forgive Saf, aren't you?"

He pursed his lips and shook his head. "I have something else to say to you."

"Okay," I said.

"You may have failed at convincing Saf."

Not what I wanted to hear, but something I couldn't dispute either.

"Or you might have gotten it right, but still do or say something that changes her mind again."

Also true. Also painful to hear.

"Or you might make other mistakes that allow Xiii to prevail. All of these possibilities are very real."

"Right," I whispered.

"You might struggle to care about a world that isn't yours."

I was pretty sure that not caring about people just because they were in a different community was a bad thing. I wasn't that bad of a person, was I?

"There are many mistakes you could make that would doom this entire realm to live under Xiii's thumb and let him win against me."

"And then we won't save Earth," I said.

"There are other ways to save Earth."

"But we'll never find them."

"I would help you find them."

I looked at him again.

He looked back at me. "I would help you save human civilization, even."

"But?" I prompted.

"But nothing." He shrugged.

"You would help us even if we completely screw up and doom your world to an eternal reign of the devil?"

"Yes. And I would forgive you. Without reservation."

That hit like a boulder to the chest. It shouldn't have surprised me. This was central to the philosophy, after all, but the difference of knowing it and feeling it was like the difference between a lawn sprinkler and a tsunami.

I could destroy this world through incompetence or negligence and never be punished for it, not even by the person who'd made this place his eternal life's work.

"Okay," I whispered. Then I considered what this meant for me. "So I need to forgive Saf. I need to put the fate of her world above my feelings about her. I need to be all in."

His smile this time was knowing.

I shut my eyes. "Because if I choose to do the wrong thing, then you can't forgive me. I'll have made my choice to defy everything you stand for and I know better..." I got to my feet, wishing I could leave, that I could go inside the house and lock the door. Well, I probably could, but I knew I shouldn't. And that was key. "Saf didn't know any better. It's not fair for me to judge her."

"Well..."

"I should forgive her. I'm supposed to forgive her. It's the morally right thing to do."

The breeze stirred again and lifted my hair off the side of my neck. Some creature moved away in the grass.

"As long as you try to do the right thing, I will forgive you," he said.

"But I've killed people," I confessed.

"You have killed one vampire."

"I helped kill Evan. I set up Melanie's death. I killed a ton of prairie dogs when we killed Evan. Those aren't people but... they were innocent."

"There are plenty of exalted people in our tradition who have killed, are there not? You have to make the best choice. There often isn't a perfect one, is there? Or even a good one. Did you make the best choice?"

I couldn't think of a better one in any of those instances.

He smiled and also got to his feet. "Do your best. It was never like you to do less than your best, don't change now."

I nodded.

He put a hand on my shoulder. It was warm and solid, nothing like the touch of a demon. "Time grows short. I will let you get on with what you need to do."

REALITY TILTED AND I saw, like a video played in double-time, Ro and Jaelyn yanking aside the boards that covered the door and hauling my limp body out. Corban wanted to carry me but Ro wouldn't allow it. He carried me himself, while my friends and Saf and Gamlat were each picked up by winged demons and everyone was flown towards the portal, which wasn't too far, I now saw.

The full moon was high in the sky, looking much bigger than it ever had on Earth. Then again, it didn't have the same features of Earth's moon. No Man in the Moon, nor the Rabbit that people in the Southern Hemisphere saw.

At the portal, there was still the huge crowd of demons trying to get through, but others had shown up as well. A horde of winged demons, that at least equalled the number waiting to go through, hovered around the ziggurat, creating a large, glowing cloud. Ro looked up at them, fearfully.

Xiii was already there, silent and hovering at the head of his own forces, who stood arrayed across the dark plain. His wings were golden now, as was his skin. His eyes looked black to me; the brown eyes he'd had before were a glamour he'd conjured up. A lie.

"Stand aside!" he thundered. "We are bringing the traitor through."

Those waiting to go through the portal turned, while those hovering overhead dove.

Wordless shouts went up as the airborne demons collided with those on the ground. As with all the fights I'd seen here, this one displayed the participants' ineptitude. None of them even knew how to throw a punch, nor did they show any of the customary norms of fair play. It wasn't even clear who was trying to accomplish what, given the mayhem.

All of them yanked hair and kicked stomachs and clawed each other's faces.

Under the light of the moon, these rudimentary blows caused plenty of pain. Demons shrieked and screamed as they lashed out in return.

Saf, flanked by Xiii's guards, held up a hand and sent a great wave of air before her, pushing aside everyone who stood between her and the portal. I would have instead gone up one of the other sides of the ziggurat, but I supposed this was more dramatic.

I had enough time to see all this, and then I was falling down and down, picking up speed as I hurtled towards my own body, lying limp in Ro's arms. He and Jaelyn and my friends were surrounded on all sides by Xiii's forces, which had also taken wing and joined the fray. I fell past them as my body recalled my consciousness to itself.

With a jolt like I'd been hit with an electric shock, I came awake in Ro's arms.

"Okay?" he asked.

I could barely hear him over the screams of the angels fighting every direction. Above and around us, the air was full of swords clashing and screams ringing out. I opened my eyes and looked up at him, expecting him to shout that I was awake and that he wanted someone to help him.

He didn't.

And after a few fractions of a second, I realized he'd untied my bonds.

"What are you doing?" I asked in a low voice. We couldn't whisper, not with all the shouting all around.

"Helping you," he said.

"Why? Are you insane?"

"Because you're right," he replied. "I heard what you said to Saf."

I stared at him.

He shrugged. "I mean... I don't know about what you were saying about morality or whatever. I never did get that."

What else had we talked about?

"Your world has the best stuff, by far," he said. "Everything here is a pale imitation. If you can make this world more like your world—"

"Okay, that is kind of beside the point of what we were arguing..."

"Do you want my help or not?" he asked.

THIRTY-SEVEN

With exaggerated care, Ro lowered me to the ground. "Stay limp, look like you're still out."

Perhaps this was a clever plot cooked up by Xiii, but it worked. I obeyed him and shut my eyes.

"Yeah?" said Jaelyn, landing beside us.

"Yeah, it's all good."

The jet black non-ground felt strange to lie on. It was like the demons themselves, solid but without much substance.

"Everyone else's bonds are cut," said Jaelyn. "So what do we do now?"

My eyes snapped open and I stared up at the two luminous faces that looked down at me. "What?" I asked.

"She really likes your house," said Ro. "Not sure we could recreate it here. Not exactly."

"Um... right." I needed allies, and there was no point judging these two.

Their help also did me no good if I didn't figure out what help I needed. "Who of the others might have told Xiii about your plans to defect?"

"They're not gonna understand what we're doing," said Jaelyn. "Unless I can recreate your house exactly, they're not gonna comprehend—"

"Fine," I cut her off. "Who else of your kind learned to fight?"

"Nobody, I don't think," said Ro. "I lied."

"You had humans with fighting skills living here for centuries."

"Well, that wasn't something people here wanted to learn," said Jaelyn.

"I mean, I taught them a little but..." Ro shrugged.

"All right." I took a deep breath. This was truly insane. "What I need is to get to Saf."

Ro nodded. "On three." He counted and then he and Jaelyn leapt to their feet.

"To me!" Ro shouted.

My friends all threw off their bonds and ran to us. Their demonic captors stood aside, gazes on Ro, who nodded at them. Only Gamlat remained bound and scowling on the ground, like a toddler assigned to time in the corner.

"Run," Ro told the other demons. He drew a sword, which glistened in the light of stars as he drew it out of the thin air. He drew a second one and tossed it to Corban.

And the other demons ran, just as Xiii swung his gaze back to us. He was easy enough to see, shining gold as he did far above.

Corban and Ro swung their swords in nearly identical figure eights, getting used to the balance of them.

"We need to get her to Saf," said Ro.

Corban looked at me for confirmation.

I nodded. "Please."

"Why is he helping us?" Corban asked

"I'll explain later."

Saf was halfway up the ziggurat by now, with the legions of demons closing in behind her. That meant there was no way to get to her without slashing our way through.

Amy and Gina huddled together behind me. "We're getting out of here, right?" I heard Amy say. Her speaking voice was hard to hear over the cacophony of shouts and screams.

Jaelyn spread her wings and leapt upwards, using strong wingbeats to climb up through the ranks of those fighting above us.

"Let's go!" I shouted.

Ro and Corban nodded at each other and spun into action. They ran for the base of the stairs, and I followed, glancing back to make sure my friends followed.

They were not letting me go anywhere without them. They stayed right on my heels.

At the base of the ziggurat, Corban and Ro began their grisly work, cleaving a way through the press of bodies. While many of those waiting on the stairs had taken wing, those who remained were locked in battle, and the push and pull of the fight took up all the space. Everyone cleared aside to dodge the blades, though some weren't quick enough to avoid a slash or a cut. I averted my eyes and focused on climbing the first few stairs.

Something wet hit my cheek and I rubbed at it with my hand, which came away bloody.

Amy gave me a startled look. "Are you okay?"

"It's not mine."

Another drop hit. That's when I noticed that where Ro and Corban's swords slashed through flesh, clear liquid flowed. It had been when snatching his sword back that Corban had splattered me with some of it.

Some splashed off Ro's sword, onto me, turning again to blood. While the demons themselves felt insubstantial, this fluid felt warm and wet.

A drop fell from above and I looked up.

One of the angels in flight overhead had conjured his own sword and was hacking sloppily at the others that hovered near him. More swords were appearing in hands all around, and the sound of metal clashing against metal added itself to louder, more prolonged shrieks of agony.

At least the clear fluid appeared to evaporate before hitting the stairs. They were still climbable, when on Earth they would have been slick. I paid attention to climbing and wondered if I should hold my friends' hands.

No, not while I was getting blood all over me. More splashes hit. I was sure was starting to look like I'd participated in the Texas Chainsaw Massacre. Innocent beings who may have never seen a sword in their lives were scrambling to get away as

Corban and Ro cut a path, working in perfect unison, while Xiii bellowed, "Stop them! Stop them, now!" overhead.

He didn't try to intervene himself, though. Even more telling was how many angels crowded in, trying to block our path. Xiii making them do the dirty work didn't seem to give them pause.

I wanted to look back at my friends, but I couldn't pause, nor could I take my eyes off where I was going. This staircase was steep, and the steps shallow. "You guys okay?" I shouted instead.

"Don't worry about us," was Amy's reply.

I'd known Corban was a soldier and seen him fight before, but not quite like this. Slaughtering vampires and the humans who tried to kill him was one thing, this was different. He moved like a machine, precise, deadly, and untiring.

Warm blood now ran in rivulets down my cheeks and arms and its coppery reek made me dizzy. I was walking through a nightmare.

And yet, I had to keep walking. There might have been other ways to save human civilization on Earth, but this was the only way to save both worlds.

On I climbed, wishing I could see how close we were to Saf, but with all the fighting and chaos all around, that wasn't possible. This was war, and some of the first violence these beings had ever known. Tears ran down my face, mixing with the blood that now soaked my clothes and hair, weighing down my every step.

Just keep climbing, I told myself.

WE REACHED THE top of the platform after what felt like ten hours of climbing, though it could have been two or five or fifteen for all I knew. I'd been praying to be done since the first minute of the slaughter.

The fact that we reached the top without overtaking Saf made my pulse race, but she hadn't gone through the portal yet.

Corban and Ro parted to let me through.

Saf had stopped walking and turned around.

Behind her, standing where the arch used to be, with her wings outstretched, was Jaelyn. So this was where she'd gone. Her expression was determined, though I doubted she could have lasted five minutes against Saf.

As I stepped onto the level stone, I realized I wasn't soaked with blood anymore. My clothes and skin felt dry, clean, and fresh like they'd never encountered a single drop.

I looked back over my shoulder and saw, much to my relief, Gina and Amy ascending to the platform as well. Their lack of surprise made me wonder if I'd imagined the whole blood-shower.

Saf was waiting, her expression unreadable. "What is it?" she demanded.

"Get back!" Xiii roared.

I'd gotten so used to his shouting in the background that I'd come to ignore it. Now, though, I realized it meant he'd followed me. No longer content to let others fight his fight, he dove at me.

I held up one hand, unsure of what I could do to fend him off.

But he stopped. His wings were still folded, his hands balled into fists, but he hung in the sky like a fly trapped in amber. His open mouth yielded no sound.

Around us, demons dropped their weapons with soft clangs.

The world was going quieter again, and not because the moon had left. It still hung in the sky, nearing the horizon but not likely to encounter it for another hour or more.

It was as if the very realm itself held its breath, waiting for what I would say.

THIRTY-EIGHT

I didn't feel prepared for this, but I supposed that would have been the case even if I'd climbed for half of eternity.

Sorry... I suppose nerdy jokes about half of eternity (which is also eternity) aren't appropriate at a time like this.

Saf fixed her black gaze on me and I willed my words not to catch in my throat.

"I forgive you, all right?" That came easily enough, and yet, it didn't carry the power that it had when this world's creator had said it to me. That's because I was, relatively speaking, nobody.

Saf looked appropriately unimpressed.

Forgiveness was what I had to do for me. What was I supposed to do for her? I'd been thinking about this during most of the climb, and I felt as inadequate as I had when I'd begun. There was a reason I was here, though. I had to tell her the things only I could know, being from Earth. As the last tamer of demons for my world, I had to teach her how to be the first for hers.

"You... you have the chance to free all of them." I gestured around at her people, who filled the sky.

Her expression remained unreadable.

"The tamer of demons will set them free," I said. "Do this and they'll get to live their own lives and make their own choices."

"And take consequences," she said.

"It's worth it. Don't run from this. Don't end your life before it's even begun."

"To live is to suffer." She folded her arms. She still thought this was about revenge, and that I was trying to trick her into becoming capable of pain and loss. Eve had certainly suffered her fair share of those.

"Sometimes life does mean suffering," I said.

She smirked at me. Her expression was arrogant and condescending and made me want to slap her.

I took a step forward.

She didn't move a muscle as I walked, stopping only when we were toe-to-toe. She was taller than I was, and her eyes, though black, didn't seem quite so empty now. Looking into them I could see doubt and fear.

"I have suffered," I said, my words clipped. "I miss my dad. I wish I'd never met Evan, and there are people on Earth who have it much, much worse."

"But it's okay?" she asked, her voice dripping with sarcasm. "Because it's less boring than paradise?"

"It's not okay," I said, "and it never will be. I'm okay, though. People can hurt each other in my world, yeah. People can torture each other. Terrible things happen. And we can move on. You wouldn't have any idea how to do that, so this superior act you've put on..." I shook my head. "It shows you know nothing. You spent thousands of years on Earth and didn't earn one scrap of wisdom."

Okay, I told myself. Dial it back. Saying I forgave her was the easy part. I needed to actually do it, and that meant not insulting her.

Her grin grew more triumphant. "You'd be correct that I don't understand why deciding you don't care about your father anymore is some great feat of humanity."

"That's not how it works. I'll always love my dad."

"But you love me now too? So it balances out?" She was still being sarcastic, but her confusion was also real. She did not understand what I was saying.

"Well... I love you in a deep, spiritual way, I guess." I sighed. "Not like I love my dad, no."

Her gaze searched mine, and the mask of confidence slipped.

She tried to convince me that she was right by being arrogant. I didn't need to play that same game. Rather than act haughty, I simply said my truth.

The truth.

"Once you are able to feel loss and pain, you learn what you're really made of." I waved my hand to indicate her whole body. "This is a pale shadow of what you really are. This kingdom is a pale shadow of who your people really are and what they can accomplish, but you've got to be brave enough to take the next step. There is so much you do not understand."

At those words, her gaze shifted to over my shoulder, her lips pursing and the confusion in her eyes more naked.

"Like having friends," Gina quipped. "People who'll put up with you without being forced."

Silly as that insult seemed, it hit home. Saf recoiled.

"Love is one of those things she can't understand yet," said Corban. He stood a few paces off, watching us. "Selfless love. Stuff that goes beyond ego strokes and strategic alliances—"

"Well, you loved your sisters, right?" I said. "You sacrificed for them."

She looked at me, baffled.

"You miss them, don't you?" I pressed.

Her gaze went back to my friends. "They would not have walked off the end of the world for me."

Was that true? I wondered. "They tried to get you back."

"Let me guess," said Corban. "Because of what you could do for them. Because of what you could accomplish together. I'm betting you never sat around braiding each other's hair and painting your toenails."

"We don't do that either, Corban," Amy snapped.

But I chuckled. "Discussing textbooks, then," I said. "And eating tamales. You think our world has the best stuff. I was really rich there, but what I spent money on was what really mattered: time and travel to be with my friends and family, my education, my relationship." I glanced at Corban. "Which is how I managed to stay a half-turned vampire. Those things are all invisible to you, aren't they? You couldn't even see the best things that exist on Earth."

She looked away.

I waited, wondering what her next insult would be.

But what she said was, "I've felt pain, you know, when I had a human body."

"Yeah, of course."

"I've felt disappointment and ecstasy, hunger and satiation. I've been hated, loved, and worshipped."

"Yeah... well..." I shrugged. "Have you ever loved anyone but yourself?"

"I am sacrificing myself for this world. Sacrificing yourself for others is central to what you believe in, is it not? Isn't it an act of love?"

"It can be," I said.

"Sometimes..." said Corban. "Or it can be selfish. Sometimes you have to die for what you believe in, but usually you have to live for it. You give your life minute by minute, choice by choice."

"Suffering by suffering," said Saf.

"No," I said. "I mean, sometimes you suffer, sure, but living for something is a good thing to do. It makes the days worth it in a way you've never understood."

She blinked, then looked down.

I held out my hand.

She stared at it for a moment, then reached out her own so that I could clasp her ghostly palm against mine. Slowly, she lifted her gaze back to my face.

What I saw made my heart break. Terror that reminded me of how I'd felt the moment I'd learned my father had died. I hadn't wanted to get out of bed the next morning, or the morning after.

I'd stared ahead at an existence so bleak, I wished it would end. She was staring into her own abyss. This situation asked her to step into a new world that only we could illuminate for her.

I pulled her into my arms. "Hey, you'll be all right. You'll be more than all right. I never got to meet the first tamer of demons for my world, but if I could, this is what I'd tell her. Thank you. Everything good in my life is because of you."

Amy and Gina and Corban all stepped up, patting her insubstantial arms and back.

"Yeah, and hey, we do love you, all right?" said Amy. "Even if we haven't always liked you. We stepped off the end of our world for you, too, you know?"

Saf's chest heaved in a sob.

And then, she was gone. I opened my eyes and lowered my arms.

Jaelyn folded her wings, uncertain. Then her eyes widened as she looked past me.

We all turned around. The demons around and above us all pivoted. The far horizon was lightening, far brighter than presaged the rising of the moon.

As we all watched, a new sun rose. It painted the black sky blue as its first rays obscured stars that had shone over this world since the beginning of time. The demons began to disappear, fading away like illusions. I looked up as Xiii winked out of existence with a soft pop.

I spun around just in time to see Ro and Jaelyn disappear. If I'd known that this was the last I'd ever see of them, I would have said goodbye. Corban put a hand on my arm, likely thinking the same thing. But things were shifting fast, now. The stone platform under us jolted, as if it were unstable.

A glance back showed me the sun was changing the realm, illuminating a green land, lush with trees and vegetation. The stone platform jolted again, nearly knocking me over.

"Get through the portal," I shouted. I grabbed Amy and Gina each by the wrist and dragged them forward. "Let's go!"

Together the four of us ran forward as the stone beneath us shifted and the world went dark once more.

AND THEN SUNLIGHT hit my eyes again, but it was a dappled sunlight. We were under the outstretched branches of a large tree, its roots snaking through the buckled and broken pavement on which we now stood. The air was saturated with the scent of mulch and moisture and diesel and rust. Scents I'd barely noticed before going to a world that had been devoid of them.

All four of us had made it.

Amy and Gina even looked around with recognition.

"Oh, hey," said Gina. "We're back here."

This, then, must have been where Aline had brought them. It roughly matched Gina's description.

Corban stepped over to me and wrapped an arm around my waist. "You all right?" he asked.

"I think so. You?"

He kissed my temple. "Yeah." He had a little scruff on his chin that rubbed against my skin like sandpaper.

Women were piling out of one of the doors of the rundown apartment building.

"You're back," one of them said, her accusatory tone made all the more cutting by her German accent.

"We are," said Gina. "This is Liana and Corban."

"Ah... right. Well, I guess that explains it." The woman, a blond with fair skin, shielded her eyes and looked me over. "Welcome."

"Is Aline here?" I asked.

"No... she is in another realm. Somewhere with a better hospital."

"Is the plague over?" Amy asked.

"It is, of course, yes. It's been two months since the portal closed and the angels and vampires all returned to mortality."

"Two months?" asked Gina.

The metal door-cover creaked open again, and my Aunt Cassie stepped out.

"What... how..." I let go of Corban and ran to her, throwing my arms around her.

She was still stick thin, but she hugged back with real energy, and laughed. "You're alive. I am glad. I am so glad," she said. "Taos... The entire valley... I don't want to talk about it."

The German woman interjected in a way that showed she knew my aunt pretty well. She changed the subject at once. "Aline demanded we get her after you two disappeared. And some of the other former angels. They're all... those who survived continue to recover. The plague wasn't kind."

"Siobhan and Mouse?" Corban asked.

"With Aline, in a city called Barraca. Best medical technology humanity has to offer. If they can survive, they will. Aline also left us instructions for us to obtain a car from Southampton, New York. A blue Toyota RAV4?"

"What?" I asked.

"Please tell me you didn't risk any lives to get it..." said Corban.

"Right," I agreed, quickly.

But the woman shook her head. "No, no. We are still arguing with what is left of the angelic order about it. Is it your car?"

"It's mine," said Corban.

"Mine," I corrected him. "The title is in my name."

Gina put a hand on my arm, which seemed like an extreme reaction to a joking fight.

But then I realized she wasn't even listening. Turning around, I saw that everyone else in the courtyard was staring at something I couldn't see. I sidled up to Amy and Gina to get a better look.

There, on the other side of the tree—hiding behind the tree, in fact—was Gamlat. She looked like she expected us to all break out rifles and shoot her.

Gina and Amy gave me dubious looks.

But I was so far past holding grudges. I'd come through this ordeal with my health, best friends, boyfriend, single remaining family member, and car. What hit me instead was a wave of guilt. I hadn't even thought about Gamlat as we fled the former Starlight Kingdom. "Hey," I said. "You made it out safe."

She looked from me to the German woman, to Amy and Gina.

"This is Gamlat," I explained to everyone from the compound.

There were expressions of shock and even a little dismay, but after a moment to compose herself, the German woman stepped forward and held out a hand. "I'm Katarina. Welcome."

"My sisters?" Gamlat asked.

"Uh... They're gone... I killed Darissa," I confessed.

"And I killed Melanie," said my aunt. "And I'm not sorry."

"It was a group effort," I said.

"But I killed her." Cassie folded her arms. "With a blow torch. He wasn't getting it done." She pointed at Corban.

"Nobody's going to hurt Gamlat," I ordered. "Clean slate, people."

Gamlat, though, was looking Cassie over, and for a tense moment I wondered if she'd lunge at her.

The tension broke when she laughed. "Sounds like quite a story."

Cassie looked back at her with narrowed eyes. "I'm Cassie Linacre," she said. "I'm what passes for an expert in off-grid technologies around here. You able to help with that?"

"I do not know what this 'grid' is that you speak of," Gamlat confessed.

"Excellent. You sound like my kind of woman," said Cassie. "Come on, then. They're going to want to talk about what happened to our old home. I'm going to hide from that conversation."

She was already halfway across the courtyard.

Gamlat didn't hesitate. With a nod to all of us, she hitched up her skirts and followed my aunt through another door and out into the sunlight.

"It's... we're having trouble with the septic system," Cassie said. "Your clean slate can start after you unclog the pipe."

Corban cracked up.

"Yeah, okay," I said. "It's good to be home."

But Amy and Gina looked stricken. Katarina had a hand on each of their backs.

Corban slipped an arm around me. "Okay," he said, "Tell us the damage."

"Taos," said Katarina, "is gone. The city, the pueblo, your families who were there, everything."

I held out my arms to my friends as they both began to sob.

THIRTY-NINE

It took us several months to track down Micah Hulsman, Aline's teen husband. None of the coyote-shifters or their mundane allies knew anything about him. His phone, I later learned, had been stolen.

The world still reeled and a third of the population of the US was dead or missing. Once great cities had been reduced to rubble and it had taken the government three weeks to get the electric grid back online. The President and Vice President had survived, as had most of Congress. Politician jokes aside, this was a good thing.

Within a month, and with the help of the surviving state governments, they'd recruited a workforce to begin rebuilding infrastructure, paying people in cheap, surplus food. It helped to be a country that grew enough to feed the world. Farmland was divvied up so that planting was done in time for us to get a harvest that year.

Micah, we discovered, was enrolled in college in Nebraska, which had escaped much of the worst of the carnage, thanks in no small part to the legacy of the Kansas mages. The area even had cell phone service. We contacted him via calling the dorm phone and having someone write a note on his door.

He met me in a coffee shop that also served as a message center for refugees still seeking family and vice versa. The walls were covered with notice boards, which in turn were plastered with notices. Pushpins were dotted thick as speckles on a hen and the papers were stacked so deep that they threatened to fall like a cascade of giant snowflakes at any moment.

The place was crowded, of course, with people clutching their cups of third rate coffee (probably left over military rations) and scanning the walls, lifting up sheets of paper to read those underneath. Most people also had phones to their ears and were talking in low, earnest tones. For the world to heal, humanity would need to knit together again the bonds that made civilization possible.

The air was thick with the scent of coffee grinds and sweat. A far cry from the upscale coffee shop vibe of old.

Corban had come with me, of course. He refused to leave my side. Our wedding rings were still shiny and new, though our running joke that it was the only way to resolve who got to keep the RAV4 was getting old. That car was as reliable as ever. It had gotten us here from the coyote-shifter compound (which it turned out was in Arizona.)

Right now Corban was helping a woman with dwarfism and a wicked sense of humor read the notices set too high for her to reach.

He still attracted plenty of female attention, though he considered himself very different looking than he'd been as an angel. Our arguments about who had changed less were also getting old. Furthermore, he refused to see my non-model figure and muddy brown eyes as downgrades.

Micah was easy to spot. He walked with a limp and still had a bandage covering his left arm up to his collarbone.

I hadn't known Aline well, but it nevertheless was clear to me what she liked about this boy. In the bustling chaos of this place, he was his own island of calm, as if he were slightly out of phase with the world, peering at the insanity from the calm of his own private nether-realm.

Living with the coyote-shifters, though, I'd learned that this trait was associated with an utter lack of supernatural potential. Micah was what was called a "true mundane." No matter what world he was portalled to, he would remain a regular, basic human. No powers, no weird physiology, just the same guy.

His eyes were a striking gray and his skin was ruddy. The heat from this overcrowded room brought out red splotches on his cheeks. His hair flopped forward, giving him cover when he was shy, I suspected. When he saw me, he tipped his head forward and regarded me through his bangs. I waved and he picked his way across the room.

I'd managed to snag a table for two, and he took a seat across from me, his whole demeanor wary.

"Hi, Micah," I said. "I'm Liana."

He didn't reply, only looked me over.

"So—"

"You know Aline?" he asked.

"Yeah."

He went silent.

It was impossible to tell whether he didn't like me, or was still angry with Aline. Perhaps it was both. His expression was closed; his eyes narrowed.

I had no idea what to say to him. All my scripted comments fled from my mind.

Finally he asked, "Did she survive?"

"Yes," I said. "But she's in a very remote location. She was one of the victims of the plague in the Middle East," I said.

"In the Middle East?" His eyebrows shot up.

I nodded. "I'm not sure how much you want to know about what happened?"

He turned his gaze away, focusing on the red canvas shoes of the woman at the next table over. After a moment, he looked at me again. "Is she ever coming back?"

Again, I couldn't read him well enough to know whether he would consider this a good or a bad thing.

"That's the plan," I said. "It may take a long time, though." The severing of the Starlight Kingdom had affected all the other worlds too. The nether-world had contracted violently, destroying the hospital. Portals had shifted by hundreds of miles and more. The portal in the world where Aline, Siobhan, and Mouse recovered was now under the ocean on their end and in the Antarctic on ours. Getting anyone through it was going to be an engineering nightmare.

Micah put his hands on the table. It was his left hand that was bandaged, so I assumed he wasn't wearing his wedding ring, but he was wearing a ball chain around his neck, like Aline had. Perhaps he just wasn't wearing the ring on his finger.

I began to doubt the wisdom of finding him. Since Aline was the only person I knew who'd ever met this guy, I had practically nothing to go on. "I'm not sure what you'll want to know," I said.

He considered that a moment, then said, "Can you... tell me if you find out that she's dead?"

"Yes, of course."

"Will you know?"

I nodded. "Eventually, yeah."

He looked me over again. "Is anyone coming after me?" he asked.

"You mean Tobias or—"

"Yeah."

I shook my head. "No. Nobody from Aline's life that we know of is after you. If you've got personal mob connections or anything like that, I can't speak to those."

His eyes twinkled with amusement. "Okay."

He left, then, without looking back, eeling his way through the crowd with easy grace.

Corban, who'd been watching from a few feet away, came to take his chair. "Well?" he asked.

I shrugged. "I guess it went as well as could be expected."

Micah stood for a moment, silhouetted in the doorway, and then he slipped out and was gone.

Corban took my hand. "Aline will be back."

I nodded. In the meantime, the ragtag group of juvenile coyote-shifters and their adult carers needed our support. "How do you feel about me going to med school?" I asked.

"Are there any left standing?"

"Arizona's announced it'll take a new class. I bet I could get in."

"Sounds good," he said. He took every suggestion I made with equanimity, as if it were all no big deal.

I suppose after the existence he'd already had, it wasn't.

"Let's go," I said.

"Amy texted me, wondering when we'll be back."

"Lie to her. You're not an angel anymore."

He lifted an admonishing eyebrow at me.

"Then stall," I amended.

There was no point telling Amy what we were up to, not yet. She still did not want to talk about the loss of her family and people, and I couldn't blame her.

Jack Naranjo, Amy's beloved—whom I'd caught her crying over pictures of—was not from Taos, though, but rather the Española Valley. This area had only flooded. There had been survivors. New Mexico was between us and the coyote-shifter compound and there was no way I was driving across it without stopping to search for him.

My friends had gone to the end of the world and beyond for me. There was nothing I wouldn't do for them.

Thanks so much for reading!
These characters will be back in future books.

ACKNOWLEDGMENTS

I write these acknowledgments while recovering from a whole lot of health problems, which means typo-catchers were more vital than ever. First thanks always goes to Dr. Char Peery, who typically has excellent taste in books, but also reads my rough drafts. An invaluable friend indeed!

The valiant typo-catchers deserve a huge shout out, because there were a ton of typos in this one. I wrote part of this from the hospital, a lot of it from my sickbed, and had to take time off when medication side-effects were destroying my ability to form complete sentences. Thus, I owe a huge thanks to Trish Duffel, Sharon Ayers, Jeff Ney-Grimm, Jordan Spencer, Viola Braxmaier, Karie Crawford, and others who prefer not to be named. My mother and husband deserve an extra heartfelt thank you; they were typo catching right up to the bitter end.

Thanks also goes to Critical Mass, my writer's group, who are: S.M. Stirling, Lauren Teffeau, Sarena Ulibarri, S.E. Burr, Rebecca Roanhorse, John Jos. Miller, and J. Barton Mitchell.

A final read through and honest critique was provided by Jane Lindskold, powering me through the very final draft.

Then there's always the formatting team. The cover was designed by me and Linda Caldwell, and Tara Jones, Tianne Samson, and Stacey Tippetts round out the team at E.M. Tippetts Book Designs. All the prettiness of these books is thanks to them.

And as always, I want to thank my family. The Sunrise Prophecy was over a year in the making, and while I planned far ahead to make my deadlines, my health conspired against me. My parents, husband, boys, and church community supported me over the finish line, and I am eternally grateful!